When They Fall In Love

A Novel by
Mary Lydon Simonsen

www.austenauthors.net
http://marysimonsenfanfiction.blogspot.com

Printed in the United States of America
Published by Quail Creek Publishing LLC in collaboration with White Soup Press
quailcreekpub@hotmail.com

©2013 Quail Creek Publishing LLC
ISBN 13: 978-0615790053
ISBN 10: 0615790054

Dedication

This novel is dedicated to Jakki Leatherberry, editor extraordinaire, who poked, prodded, and pulled a better story out of me. Without her, this novel would have been very different.

Chapter 1

While holding the hand of her young charge, Elizabeth Bennet sheltered with Cassandra Bingley in a cloister in Aix-en-Provence. Earlier in the day, while visiting the Cathedral of Sainte Savior in the ancient Roman city, a monk had pointed out the beauties of the sanctuary dedicated to the Redeemer and had offered to show a group of English tourists the nearby cloister. While the tour was in progress, the drizzle that had been falling all morning had turned to rain, and the storm's bounty cascaded off the roof and on to the courtyard and the garden at its heart.

Gently tugging on her Aunt Elizabeth's hand, little Cassie asked if she might be permitted to walk the gallery embracing the monks' gardens. Elizabeth saw no harm in it. After all, it would be impossible to leave the cloister until the rain eased, so why not allow the five-year-old to exercise her little legs. Although it was important for the child to have a regular schedule, it was equally important for her to be accepting of change, a hard-learned lesson from her own life.

While watching the rain splash on the cobbles that formed the perimeter of the individual garden plots, Elizabeth recalled how long it had been since she had left England: July 29, 1820 to be exact. Before boarding the ship in Brighton, she had purchased a newspaper that was filled with news of the opening of an engineering marvel, the Union Chain Bridge across the River Tweed in Scotland. As its designer was an officer in the Royal Navy, it was much spoken of amongst the ship's officers.

With a strong head wind driving the vessel back toward England, Elizabeth was still reading the same paper two days later when the packet ship arrived at Dieppe, their portal into France. With *terra firma* clearly in sight, the passengers, anxious for a platform that did not move beneath them, gazed longingly at the workers scurrying about the wharves like beetles on a fallen log. After being tossed about for the whole of the voyage, the Bingley party was told that they must wait for the seas to calm as it would be necessary for them to climb down the ropes into the waiting rowboats that would carry them to shore.

During their sea trial, Elizabeth had experienced intermittent bouts of seasickness, but it was nothing compared to poor Jane's *mal de mer*. Charles had fared better than his wife and sister-in-law, but not as well as his daughter. Despite the rolling and pitching, Cassie had found her sea legs whilst still in sight of the English coast causing her father to remark that if she had been a boy, she might have had a future in His Majesty's Navy.

As her eyes made out the bobbing curls of the red-headed Cassie on the far side of the cloister, Elizabeth recalled the journey from the Channel port to Paris. When plans for the excursion had first been discussed, the French capital was to be their final destination. Even after the lapse of the agreed-upon four-month visit, Elizabeth had yet to grow tired of Paris. Unlike London, which had lost so much of its medieval past in The Great Fire, evidence of the Middle Ages could be found in every street of the Ile de la Cite, most especially in the quarter surrounding the great cathedral of Notre Dame.

On sunlit days, Elizabeth and Cassie wandered the gardens of the Tuileries, the same gardens where Marie Antoinette had spent long summer days with her children before being imprisoned in the dungeon-like Concierge. When the weather was against them, all would visit the tapestry works or the Sévres porcelain factory, but Elizabeth's favorite outing was to the Louvre. The former palace of the Bourbon Henri IV was now used to display the spoils of war wrested from a conquered Europe during the reign of Napoleon. It was very much like finding oneself a tiny creature inside a treasure box filled with the riches of the world.

Unlike Elizabeth, Jane *had* grown tired of Paris. She did not like the "over sauced" and "over spiced" French food and hated the smell of the garlic-soaked frog legs that appeared on every menu. She had had her fill of operas, plays, and balls. Even the fashion salons and Paris's famed milliners had lost their appeal. As for

Charles, he had been suited and booted to the point where his armoire was bursting with the latest fashions displayed by the Parisian tailors in their windows as well as the bootmaker's offerings.

Rather than turning north toward England, Jane had decided to act on a suggestion made by Fitzwilliam Darcy in one of his many letters to Charles that they visit the spa at Vichy. Elizabeth understood the reason for Jane's interest. Since the difficult birth of Cassie five years earlier, her older sister had not been in the best of health and had hoped that a French spa might succeed in bringing relief where the English spas at Tunbridge Wells and Buxton and sea bathing at Brighton had failed. With regard to the alteration in plans, Elizabeth made no complaint.

With most of their baggage sent ahead to their hotel, the party set out on their three-hundred-mile journey. Compared to the roads leading from the Channel ports to Paris, the byways of central France were primitive, dusty, and deserted. In order to avoid crater-sized holes in the road, it often proved necessary to get out of the carriage and walk in order to spare the horses and the springs of the carriage. The roadside inns were so inferior to the hotel suite they had leased in Paris that Elizabeth was convinced Jane would insist they abandon their plans and turn the carriage around, their destination: the nearest Channel port. Instead, the Bingleys had pressed on.

Once in Vichy, Charles found a letter waiting for him at the front desk of the hotel from Mr. Darcy, who was leasing a villa in the hills above Florence. In the letter, Darcy had suggested that after enjoying the waters of Vichy, they should go farther—much farther—to Aix-en-Provence to visit the best spa on the Riviera. Elizabeth, who believed one spa was as good as the next, had protested the addition of another two-hundred miles to an already long and arduous journey, but to Jane's argument that Mr. Darcy was an expert on the various French spas, Elizabeth had no rebuttal. Finally, her curiosity about Provence and France's famed Cote d'Azur took hold, and she thought, why not? Although lacking in fortune, she was rich in time.

After dashing off letters to her parents at Longbourn and Charlotte Collins in Kent informing them of their change in plans, Elizabeth climbed into the carriage for the start of a most wretched journey.

When the travelers arrived at their destination, the exhausted party appeared at the door of Monsieur Lavelle, who was in possession of the keys to their apartment on the Avenue of Fountains. Although they viewed the residence by candlelight, they were delighted to find themselves settled in spacious and clean rooms. In the morning, they feasted on the sight of Montagne Sainte Victorie framed within the windows of their apartment. It was while viewing the incredible mountain scenery that Jane had informed her sister that all accommodations in Aix had been arranged by Mr. Darcy.

Chapter 2

After a good soaking, the rain ceased, and the brilliant sun of the South of France returned. With umbrellas folded, Elizabeth and Cassie walked to the town center. Across from the Hotel de Ville, flower sellers circled a fountain, their wares creating a brilliantly colored wreath. Every Friday, Cassie was permitted to select a small bouquet for her mother from one of the vendors. The little girl, who had learned some of the local dialect from the cook, engaged the seller in a conversation that was as much pantomime as prose.

Although Elizabeth had been cool to the idea of going to Aix, she found that she loved the city. While Jane spent her days at a spa first enjoyed by the Romans in the early Christian era, Elizabeth saw to Cassie's lessons, and with the little girl in tow, they visited the sites. On three occasions, she had convinced Charles to hire a guide to take Cassie and her to Nîmes to see the well-preserved ancient Roman aqueduct. Near to this engineering marvel was the Maison Carrée, as perfect a temple as likely to be found in the Roman world, and a favorite of tourists who spent hours sketching it.

Even though she missed her family, most especially her dear Papa, Elizabeth was quite content to remain in Aix. Here in Provence, people were more inclined to view her as Madame's sister and not the poor relation who had never married and who had been taken into the Bingley household in Christian charity. When amongst the English, Miss Elizabeth Bennet was thought of as Cassie's governess, but in Aix, she was the child's dear aunt.

Enjoying the mild climate, Elizabeth decided there was no need to hurry back to England, especially when one considered Madame Lavelle's prediction that the rainy season was about to begin. In light of Madame's intelligence, it made sense to wait for the rains to end before setting out for Paris. If they stayed for the summer, they would have been gone from England for more than a year, a lapse of time noted by her father in his every letter.

After returning to their apartment, Elizabeth found Jane resting, something she did every afternoon after a long day spent taking the waters and visiting with a coterie of English ladies at the spa. As usual, Charles was in the study reading correspondence from home where a manor house was being built on property he had purchased about twenty miles south of the estate of his good friend, Mr. Darcy.

With Mr. Bingley's father stipulating in his will that a goodly portion of his inheritance must be spent on the building of a great house, finally, after seven years of marriage and a prolonged presence at Netherfield Park, the couple had set about doing it, supervising the construction of the manor from a leased estate near Derby. With Jane's role of decorating the interiors delayed until the completion of the exterior, Charles had suggested a trip to the Continent. Correspondence from the estate manager had followed along their circuitous route.

As soon as aunt and niece entered the study, Cassie ran to her father, who scooped his only child up in his arms. After sharing her day with him, she quickly left to go to the kitchen where a special treat awaited her. The remainder of the afternoon would be spent with Marie, a young woman from the town, who had been hired for that purpose.

"How goes the building of Bingley Hall?" Elizabeth asked while removing her pelisse, hat, and gloves.

"Very well. Very well indeed," Charles answered, his usual buoyant self. "I could not possibly have a better man running the construction of the house than Willis Rumford. If Darcy never makes another recommendation, he will have done me a great service just by telling me about Rumford."

"You say that about every suggestion Mr. Darcy makes," but then she smiled as she had no reason to doubt the sincerity *or* accuracy of Charles's statement.

"Speaking of Darcy, I have had a letter from him," he said, picking up a piece of paper from his desk. "He wants us to come to Florence so that I might go to Pistoia in July for the Palio, a race run in the middle of a medieval town! Just think of the skill required to control your horse in such a tight venue while going full out." Charles, an expert horseman, was already running the race in his mind. "What do you think about that, Elizabeth? Are you up for it?"

Elizabeth did not know what to think, her mind freezing at the mention of seeing Mr. Darcy.

"Florence," Elizabeth said, sinking into a chair. "No, I do not want to go to Florence. It is too far. When this journey was discussed, we spoke of Paris and then Vichy, and here we are in Aix. To go to Florence, would take us farther from home. No, I do not want to put any more distance between England and me."

"What about England?" Jane asked as she came into the room stifling a yawn.

"I was just mentioning to Charles that we should be thinking about our return journey home."

"I am surprised to hear it, Lizzy. At breakfast, you indicated that your preference was to remain in France at least through September."

It was true. That very morning, when Charles and Jane had mentioned leasing a villa on the Mediterranean for the summer, Elizabeth had enthusiastically endorsed the idea. Sea bathing in the warm waters of the Mediterranean would be a delight, especially when compared to the cold waters of the Channel bathing sites.

"Actually, Elizabeth and I were discussing an offer made by Darcy to join him in Tuscany," Charles informed his wife. "You may recall that Darcy is currently leasing a villa outside Florence. According to this letter, the house is large enough to accommodate us all."

"Florence?" Jane said, shaking her head. "The idea of riding in a carriage day after day and staying in dilapidated roadside inns has little appeal for me."

There was also the problem of Jane traveling without a lady's maid. As soon as the maid had heard that the Bingleys would be setting out from Vichy for Aix, and not Derbyshire, she had insisted they make arrangements for her to return to England. Jane, who had grown used to having an attendant, missed her maid, and Elizabeth's efforts to serve as a substitute had proved less than ideal.

"We would not go by carriage," Charles said. "Darcy has written that the best way to travel to the Italian peninsula is by ship."

"Another sea voyage!" Jane said and made a face, reminding Elizabeth of just how ill her sister had been whilst aboard the packet ship from Brighton to Dieppe.

From her sister's initial response, Elizabeth, who was opposed to the idea, felt she had a powerful ally in Jane. If history served as a guide, Charles would give in to his wife.

"Now that I think about it, as soon as I arrived in Dieppe, I was fine," Jane said, completely reversing her position. "Is there a spa nearby?"

"Knowing you would ask, Darcy mentioned a place called Bagno Vignoni, not too far from Florence. He writes that the site was enjoyed by the Romans who consecrated the waters to the Nymphs. Sounds interesting," Charles said with arched eyebrows.

While Charles assured his wife that she would have access to the thermal waters she found necessary to the preservation of her health, Elizabeth's mind was a muddle. It was not Florence she wished to avoid, but their host, Mr. Darcy!

"The arrangements for such a journey would require a good deal of... a good deal of planning and...," Elizabeth said, stuttering a protest.

"That is true," Charles answered. "Fortunately, on our behalf, Darcy contacted Mr. Eldridge who manages the Bingley warehouses in Leghorn. Because a ship travels regularly between the ports of Livorno, as the Tuscans call it, and Marseille, we shall go on one of our own ships and the carriage as well! So what is it to be, ladies? Are we up for an adventure?"

Elizabeth shook her head so violently that a curl was released from its pins.

Jane was puzzled by her sister's response. "Lizzy, it was you who said that Florence is the greatest repository of art in the world, and everyone knows how much you love art. We could hardly tear you away from the Louvre."

"Yes, but the Louvre is in Paris, which is nearer to the Channel and home. Papa has written that he longs for our return, and Mama…"

"Charles, what is the name of that gallery in Florence that Mrs. Morgan is always mentioning?" Jane asked, ignoring Elizabeth's commentary.

Charles shook his head in ignorance. Art was definitely not his subject, and he never listened to Mrs. Morgan, a self-proclaimed authority on everything, no matter the subject.

"The Uffizi," Elizabeth answered.

"Yes, that is it! The gallery is supposed to have some of the greatest paintings and sculptures of the Italian Renaissance."

"Very well, I shall go," Elizabeth said, standing up. "Because I am dependent upon you for my every need, I must agree to any plan you propose." With that, she gathered up her things and hurriedly left the room.

Chapter 3

After fleeing the study, Elizabeth quickly made her way down to the kitchen where Cassie was enjoying a sweet with Marie. Following a quick pat on the child's head, she went through the servants' door to the rear entrance where the merchants delivered their wares. With a few coins in her reticule, she took aim for a tea shop that had been established to cater to the increasing number of tourists who were coming to Aix for health reasons and to escape the cold English winters and the vagaries of an English summer.

With a nod, the owner signaled that she would brew a pot of Elizabeth's favorite tea to be accompanied by a plate of seed sable biscuits, a local specialty that Elizabeth would miss when she returned home—*if* she returned home. *At this rate, I might very well end up in Constantinople*, Elizabeth brooded.

After taking a sip of the tea, she closed her eyes in an attempt to settle her mind. What was to be done? If Jane and Charles were determined to go to Florence, she must go with them, with the result being that she would be Mr. Darcy's houseguest. Although she had been in that gentleman's company since that awful day at the Hunsford Parsonage when she had refused his offer of marriage, this was different. It was one thing to see Mr. Darcy in the midst of a crowd at a social gathering at Netherfield Park, but quite another to see him every day, for weeks on end, in his own villa. There was another consideration. The last time she had been in his company, Mr. Darcy was married, but now he was a widower!

Elizabeth gazed out of the shop window. Although the square was filled with people going in and out of the shops, she saw only blurs. Instead, the image impressed on her mind was of the parlor at Hunsford. Not only had she refused Mr. Darcy's offer, but she had done so in such a way that she had merited a strong rebuke from her rejected suitor: "I might, perhaps, wish to be informed why, with so little endeavor at civility, I am thus rejected. But it is of small importance."

"Yes, Mr. Darcy, it *was* of small importance because if it had not been, it would have been impossible for you to transfer your affections to another within a matter of months of my refusal," she said, unaware that her words had been uttered aloud.

"Is anything wrong, Madame?" the shopkeeper asked in imperfect English.

"No, nothing is wrong." *Or at least nothing that can be remedied.*

Elizabeth's thoughts turned to another scene: Mr. Darcy and his wife, Amelie Cantwell, the setting, a supper at Netherfield Park. As was to be expected of the wife of a man such as Fitzwilliam Darcy of Pemberley, Elizabeth knew that Mrs. Darcy would be pretty, but she was much more than that. She was perhaps the most beautiful woman Elizabeth had ever seen, and with her blonde hair, blue eyes, alabaster skin, and tall silhouette, in every way different from Elizabeth Bennet of Hertfordshire.

The couple had only just returned from a lengthy visit to the Continent with their daughter, a cherubic two-year-old with golden hair. While the elegant Mrs. Darcy conversed with Mr. Bingley's sisters, Mr. Darcy showed Elizabeth a miniature of his little girl, clearly his pride and joy, and even though the exercise brought with it its own discomfort, she was grateful for the diversion. Without the miniature on which to focus her attention, Elizabeth would have been at a loss for words. What did one say to a man whose offer of marriage she had rejected, especially when one's opinion of the man had undergone a radical change? With her pride demanding that she give no hint of her feelings, feelings she had gone to great lengths to suppress, Elizabeth had been excessive in her praise, so much so that Mr. Darcy had given her an look. Even for the proud father, her acclamations were too much!

Over the years, because Charles and Mr. Darcy were faithful correspondents, Elizabeth had been regularly updated on news concerning Mr. and Mrs. Darcy. From Charles's iteration of his friend's letters, Elizabeth knew that Amelie Darcy suffered from poor health. In an attempt to find a cure, the couple had traveled to the spas and medical centers of France before settling in Florence. It was there that Mrs. Darcy had passed away in the winter of the previous year from the influenza that had affected most of Western Europe.

Elizabeth looked down at the plate of biscuits. Lacking an appetite, she placed them in a handkerchief for Cassie. After paying Madame, she walked into the village center and headed for the apartment where she knew Jane would be waiting.

Chapter 4

"Lizzy, where have you been?" Jane asked in a voice filled with concern.

"It is a perfectly lovely day, and so I went for a walk," Elizabeth calmly answered. During her walk from the café, she had attempted to clear her mind so that she might hide the emotional upheaval going on inside her. Jane, who knew her better than anyone, quickly penetrated her façade.

"Your leaving had nothing to do with the weather," Jane said, and Lizzy could hear the hurt in her voice. "You implied that you are at the mercy of our decisions. You have never said anything like that before, and I want to know why you are saying it now."

Without giving further offense, Elizabeth could not tell her sister the reason she had left the room in a huff: Despite the many kindnesses of Jane and Charles, the truth was that she resented that events beyond her control, most especially the near bankruptcy of her father, had cost her her independence.

With the end of the wars on the Continent, the prices for grain and livestock had plummeted resulting in severe financial reversals for Thomas Bennet and his Meryton neighbors. In order to save Longbourn, it had been necessary to tap every resource, including the meager sums that had been set aside for the dowries of the unmarried Bennet daughters. In order to further ease her father's financial burden, Elizabeth had accepted an invitation from Jane and Charles to live with them, first at Netherfield Park, and then at their leased estate near Derby. Even though the pair was kindness itself, she bristled at the thought that she was dependent upon them for everything.

Years earlier, when she had heard news of Charlotte Lucas's engagement to Mr. Collins, Elizabeth had been dismissive of her friend's reasons for accepting the rector's proposal, including her wish not to be a burden to her parents or brothers and her desire to maintain her own household. According to Charlotte, marriage was the only provision for a well-educated young woman of small fortune, and however uncertain of giving happiness, must be viewed as being the most acceptable preservative from want.

In the end, with Charlotte the mistress of her own home, it had turned out that her friend had been wiser than she. With each day a reminder of what she had given up by refusing Mr. Darcy, the irony of her situation was not lost on her. *She*, not Charlotte, was the unmarried sister without an income. *She* was the spinster aunt seeing to the care of her niece. *She* was the one whose life would be determined by the decisions of others.

"Why do you not want to go to Florence?" Jane said, interrupting her sister's reverie. "Does this have anything to do with the person issuing the invitation?"

"If given a choice, I would rather not be in Mr. Darcy's company for what may turn out to be a lengthy period of time," Elizabeth answered honestly.

"I did not realize that you continued to harbor ill feelings."

"Any enmity I once felt in connection with Mr. Darcy has long since given way."

"Then I am completely confused. If there are no hard feelings, then why are you so determined to avoid his company? You have no interest in him." From the expression on Elizabeth's face, Jane realized she was wrong. "You regret having refused Mr. Darcy's offer of marriage?" Elizabeth nodded. "Then why have you not said?"

"What is there to say? Mr. Darcy proposed; I refused. He married another and fathered a child. It is as much in the past as one of those Roman ruins I visit."

"When did you change your mind about Mr. Darcy?" Jane asked, surprised by her sister's revelation.

The alteration in her opinion of the Master of Pemberley had begun within a few weeks of Elizabeth's return to Longbourn from Kent and came as a result of small, incremental changes. After several re-readings of the letter Mr. Darcy had written to her on the day after she had rejected him, a different man emerged from its pages. Yes, he was still proud, but not so proud as to have Charles Bingley, a man whose family had earned its fortune in trade, as a friend. Although he exhibited a disdain for the feelings of others, he was not so selfish as to deny Wickham the living promised him by the elder Mr. Darcy. It was true he was aloof, but not so emotionally removed as to be spared the pain of seeing his sister's heart broken by a scoundrel. And the most important reason? Despite exhibiting the snobbery of his class, Mr. Darcy had set aside his objections in order to make Elizabeth Bennet, the daughter of a gentleman farmer, an offer of marriage. She recalled the words that had since come to haunt her: "You must allow me to tell you how ardently I admire and love you."

And what had been the gentleman's reward for declaring his most ardent love? Complete and utter rejection. Roused to resentment by his listing the "honest scruples" that had prevented him from forming any serious design on her, her initial feeling, one of sorrow at his pain, quickly gave way, and her response was so vehement that it had elicited a charge of incivility from her rejected suitor. However, with the passage of time, anger had been replaced by the realization of the enormity of what she had done in refusing Fitzwilliam Darcy of Pemberley.

After visiting his magnificent estate in Derbyshire with her Aunt and Uncle Gardiner, Elizabeth better understood Mr. Darcy's struggles. In view of his wealth and rank, he would have had to endure much criticism for his choice of wife, not just from Lady Catherine de Bourgh, but from his peers, who would have questioned the wisdom of his marrying a woman who lacked a fortune and whose situation in life was so decidedly beneath his own.

There was also a matter of a change of heart. In reviewing the history of their relationship, evidence of the love Mr. Darcy felt for her had been fleshed out. With the blinders of prejudice removed, Elizabeth recalled their dance at Netherfield Park in which he had complimented her by his attention. There were also pleasant evenings spent together at Rosings Park. She remembered one evening in particular: a time when the gentleman had stood at Lady Catherine's pianoforte, gently teasing her by declaring that he was not afraid of her, and she had teased him in her turn. Prior to that evening, she had thought him overly serious and incapable of being teased, and she remembered being puzzled by his behavior. That vignette had been preceded by a series of meetings in the park and frequent afternoon visits to the parsonage. It was only upon reflection that she realized those encounters had been a prelude to a proposal.

"Lizzy, why do you not answer?"

Elizabeth did not answer because she did not want her sister to know that her estimation of Mr. Darcy had altered drastically. While visiting Pemberley, she had learned from his servants that he was an excellent brother, kind master, generous landlord, and good neighbor. In Lambton, the Darcy name elicited praise for his support of the merchants and his kindness to those less fortunate. As a result of these testimonials,

Elizabeth's opinion had softened, and she had decided that if Mr. Darcy were ever again to propose, he would receive a different answer. But history could neither be rewritten nor the present altered. Despite the gentleman's revised marital status, nothing had changed, and because a man such as he would never consider making a second offer, she had not shared her change of heart with anyone, not even her beloved sister.

"At the time of Mr. Darcy's proposal," Elizabeth explained, "I refused to believe there was any good in him when, in fact, I now know him to be a very good man. Further evidence that I had misjudged him was provided when you shared with me the contents of his letters to Charles. It touched my heart to learn that he was willing to wander from one place to another in the hope of finding a cure for his wife and to hear news of his devotion to his daughter. I already knew of his deep attachment to his sister.

"But speaking of change," Elizabeth said, "why is it that you are so eager to visit Mr. Darcy? When we were in England, because of his influence over Charles, you were frequently critical of the man. I can still hear your complaints: 'We shall go to Paris because Mr. Darcy has suggested it.' 'We shall stay in Paris where Mr. Darcy says we must stay,' and so on. Now I ask you, why the change in *your* attitude?"

Jane could not deny the charge, and she did have her reasons for resenting Mr. Darcy's interference. During the seven years of her marriage, she had learned from

Caroline and Louisa that it had been Mr. Darcy who had convinced Charles to quit Netherfield Park. If he had succeeded in permanently separating the lovers, Jane knew she would never have recovered and most certainly would never have married. Although she understood that Caroline and Louisa had parts to play, it was Mr. Darcy's considerable sway that had resulted in their separation. Having a kind heart, she had forgiven Mr. Darcy, but forgiveness did not erase a memory.

There was yet another reason. Even with Mr. Darcy on the Continent, his influence over her husband remained undiminished. It was Mr. Darcy who had suggested which property to buy, which architect to use, which estate manager to hire. He had gone so far as to design a folly for the garden. His letters to Charles were so detailed that it was as if Charles were a son receiving instructions from a parent. When Mr. Darcy suggested the trip to Paris, she had balked at the thought of complying with yet another directive from Mr. Darcy. But all that had changed in a moment.

"Jane, what is it? What are you not telling me?" Elizabeth asked before moving in front of her sister so she could not avoid her gaze.

"It is about Lydia."

"Lydia? What has Mr. Darcy to do with Lydia?"

"As it turns out, a great deal." Gesturing to a chair, she added, "You had better sit down."

Elizabeth followed her advice and took a seat near the fireplace as Jane's comment had brought on a chill.

"It was in early spring, just about the time we were discussing our plans to go to Paris that Charles and I received yet another plea for money from Lydia."

Elizabeth knew this was not an unusual request. Due to financial pressures brought on by her growing family, Lydia Wickham was chronically short of money, and she had no qualms about asking for assistance from her sister whose husband had £5,000 a year and a generous heart.

"Charles would agree to another advance only if our sister made a detailed accounting of her income and expenses so that my husband could determine where all the money was going. And there it was under income: Mr. Darcy, £25 per quarter."

"What!" Elizabeth said, her mouth agape.

"Yes, I was as surprised as you are. It seems Mr. Darcy was involved in the negotiations between Uncle Gardiner and Wickham in London. After revealing one part of the story, Lydia told us everything. It was Mr. Darcy and not Uncle Gardiner who discharged Wickham's debts in Brighton and Meryton, and it was *he* who purchased the commission for Wickham in the regular army. He also bought Lydia's wedding clothes, Wickham's uniforms, and paid for their move to Newcastle. He went so far as to attend their wedding to make sure that Wickham kept his end of the bargain."

"But why would he do that? Mr. Darcy owed the Bennets nothing." The more details Jane shared the more confused Elizabeth became.

"Lydia insisted that Mr. Darcy was only doing what a friend ought to do, but after being pressed, she repeated something Mr. Darcy had said to Uncle Gardiner, that is, if he had made Wickham's true character known to the families of the neighborhood, the elopement would never have taken place because everyone would have known that Wickham was a scoundrel."

"And Charles knew nothing of this?"

"As hard as it is to believe, only Aunt and Uncle Gardiner knew the true story, and Mr. Darcy had exacted a promise that the role he had played not be revealed. After speaking with Lydia, Charles immediately wrote to his friend, who confirmed the whole of it, with one detail added. The £25 he pays every quarter is Lydia's alone. She must collect it from the solicitor in Newcastle so that Wickham does not know about it. It seems that Mr. Darcy's allowance is all that our sister has because Wickham spends every penny he earns on gaming and drink and I am sure other things as well," she said in disgust.

"So what you are saying is that for the past seven years, Mr. Darcy has been paying Lydia £100 per annum." Jane nodded. "I think I am going to be ill."

* * *

Believing Charles would have additional information concerning Lydia and Wickham, Elizabeth, pursued by Jane, hurried to the study where she learned even more distressing details of the sordid affair of her youngest sister's spurious elopement. As it turned out, it was not Uncle Gardiner who had discovered the pair in London, but Mr. Darcy.

"But how did Mr. Darcy know of our difficulties in the first place?" a puzzled Elizabeth asked her brother-in-law.

"You are not going to like the answer." When Elizabeth continued to hold his gaze, Charles explained that Mr. Darcy had been visiting his aunt, Lady Catherine de Bourgh, in Kent when the elopement had taken place. "Apparently, Mrs. Collins had received news of the elopement from someone at Lucas Lodge, and Mr. Collins repeated the story to Lady Catherine. Once Darcy learned of it, he immediately set out for London to look for them."

Elizabeth collapsed into a chair, not knowing whether to be embarrassed or grateful. But why would Mr. Darcy involve himself in the affairs of a family he had dismissed only a short time earlier as being worthy of criticism? She recalled his harsh words concerning the inappropriate behavior of her mother and sisters. He had even taken issue with her father. Despite the passage of so many years, the words spoken in the parsonage about her family still stung, probably because they were true.

Charles repeated Darcy's belief that he had erred by not sharing with the neighborhood Wickham's reputation as a seducer. It was his conviction that if Wickham's sordid past had been known, it would have been impossible for any woman of character to fall in love with him. There was also the possibility that Lydia would not have been permitted to go to Brighton as guests of Colonel and Mrs. Forster if Wickham's history was generally known.

Elizabeth doubted this very much. Without foreknowledge of the meanness of Wickham's character and lacking evidence of any particular regard on Lydia's part for Wickham whilst the militia was quartered in Meryton, her incessant petitions to join the Forsters in Brighton would have been granted. "We shall have no peace at Longbourn if Lydia does not go to Brighton," Mr. Bennet had said in response to Lizzy's pleas that permission for the visit be denied. "Colonel Forster is a sensible man and will keep her out of any real mischief. Luckily, she is too poor to be an object of prey to anybody," *that is, anybody with a conscience.*

"Mr. Darcy has done all this on behalf of the Bennet family, and, yet, no one knows of his efforts—no one has thanked him!"

"I can tell you Darcy took no pride in the actions he took. When he spoke of the matter, he indicated that if he had had his way, Lydia would *not* have married Wickham. However, once your father sent word to your Uncle Gardiner that the couple had his permission to marry, he considered it to be instructions to move forward. It was then that he agreed to settle Wickham's debts and to buy the commission in the regular army. Knowing Wickham's true character, he took the extra step of making arrangements to provide Lydia with a quarterly income on which her husband had no claim."

Looking at his distressed sister-in-law, Charles added, "Elizabeth, I can see that you are trying to make out Darcy's motives for his involvement in a private family affair. In order to do that, you must know that I am aware that my friend made an offer of marriage to you and that you refused him. At the time of my conversation with Darcy, months after the proposal had been made, he told me he had made a hash of things, and there was no remedy for it. As far as his intervention in Lydia's affair is concerned, everything he did on her behalf, he did because of you."

Chapter 5

Shortly after Charles's astonishing revelation, Elizabeth left the study and sought the privacy of her bedchamber. She very much wished to be alone but found Jane coming through the door behind her.

"Lizzy, do you think Mr. Darcy is still in love with you?" Jane asked as soon as the door was closed behind them. "Is that the real reason for his invitation to come to Florence?"

Without having any time to digest Charles's news about Mr. Darcy's intervention on Lydia's behalf, Elizabeth made no response. She hoped her silence would indicate that she wished to be alone with her thoughts, but Jane merely repeated her question, and a reluctant Elizabeth answered. "If Mr. Darcy were still in love with me, then he was very clever in the way he went about hiding it: marrying another and moving to the Continent."

"Please do be serious," Jane said, refusing to be diverted.

Sitting on the corner of her bed, Elizabeth struck a somber pose. "To answer your question, no, I do not believe Mr. Darcy is still in love with me. I do not think it is in a man's nature to remain constant for so long, especially when one considers that he married another. But let us go back further to the time before his marriage to Miss Cantwell. The words last spoken between Mr. Darcy and I were so bitter, so angry, and the letter he wrote so filled with vitriol, I believe Mr. Darcy 'fell' out of love with me even before he left Rosings Park. Upon reflection, I am sure he considered my rejection of his offer to be a bit of good fortune, a near escape, if you will."

"Then what did Mr. Darcy mean when he told Charles that everything he did for Lydia was because of you?"

"I think it was the gentleman's way of atoning for the wretchedness of his proposal and his unkind words about our family. Subsequent interactions support this conclusion as nothing more than pleasantries were exchanged. The only reason he engaged me in conversation at all is because he was a guest in my sister's home, and the niceties of polite society demanded it."

A vision of the last time she had seen Mr. Darcy at Netherfield Park appeared, and Elizabeth could see the gentleman standing next to his beautiful wife. He had whispered something in her ear. Soon thereafter, she had played an exquisite piece on the pianoforte. But it was the intimacy of the whispered exchanged that remained so clear in her memory.

Interrupting her sister's reverie, Jane shared her doubts that Mr. Darcy was merely observing societal niceties.

"Have you forgotten that Mr. Darcy was not married to Miss Cantwell at the time of Lydia's elopement?" Elizabeth asked her sister. "If he were still in love with me, then why marry Miss Cantwell? Why not renew his attentions?"

"Did you not tell me that when rejecting Mr. Darcy you had declared that he was the last person in the world you could ever be prevailed upon to marry?" Elizabeth nodded. Although she had shared much with Jane, she had not shared everything, including Mr. Darcy's angry response: "You have said quite enough, Madam. I perfectly comprehend your feelings and have now only to be ashamed of what my own have been." Before leaving, he had wished her health and happiness, but his demeanor and tone had said something else entirely. He wished to be rid of every reminder of what had taken place that afternoon. When he left the parsonage, he had closed the door to any future communication.

"Because you left him with no hope of your ever reconsidering his offer, he looked elsewhere for a wife," Jane continued, "and where else would he look but from amongst people of rank. It is my understanding that Amelie Darcy was the granddaughter of a French vicomte, thus making her a suitable match for the grandson of an earl. It is quite possible that theirs was a marriage of convenience between two equals."

31

"I agree there is the possibility that Mr. and Mrs. Darcy were not in love when they first married, which would not be unusual for people from their social strata, but is there any doubt that they *did* fall in love? After all, Mr. Darcy spent years roaming the Continent in a desperate attempt to find a cure for his wife's illness, and although she has been gone for over a year, he cannot find it in his heart to leave the country where she is buried."

"How do you know where Mrs. Darcy is buried?"

"I had my information from you," Elizabeth answered. Despite the seriousness of the subject, she almost had to laugh at her sister's forgetfulness. Frequently, Jane complained that she suffered from "cobwebs in her brain," and there was sufficient evidence to support her conclusion. "You learned it from Mr. Darcy's sister."

"Oh, yes! Now I remember. Georgiana Legh visited with Charles and me on her way from London to Pemberley. At that time, she mentioned that Mrs. Darcy had died in a hillside villa overlooking Florence. Because a member of the Protestant faith cannot be buried in Florence, she is buried in the Protestant cemetery in Livorno." Jane sighed. "To think Mr. Darcy cannot leave Tuscany because his wife is there, well, my goodness, I must agree that *is* very romantic."

"So may we consider this argument regarding whom Mr. Darcy loves to be settled?"

"Yes, we may," Jane answered. "But does learning about Mr. Darcy's kindness toward Lydia change your mind about visiting him in Florence?"

"Jane, why are *you* so eager to go?" a puzzled Elizabeth asked. "Until recently, your opinion of Mr. Darcy was less than favorable."

"That is true, and although I resented being the recipient of so much unsolicited advice, I must admit Mr. Darcy's suggestions are always excellent. Everything he said about Aix proved to be accurate. Why should his recommendation to visit the spa at Bagno Vignoni be any different?"

Elizabeth thought, *such praise from a woman who, before they had left England, complained of Mr. Darcy's interference. Now he is as good as the oracle at Delphi.*

"Very well. I withdraw my objection."

"I shall go directly to Charles and tell him," Jane said. "Cassie will be delighted."

Elizabeth could only hope that, in the end, she would be delighted as well.

Chapter 6

As soon as the decision was made to go to Florence, Charles sent off a letter to Mr. Porter Eldridge, the Bingley representative in Livorno. By return letter, its author advised Charles to go to the French port city of Marseille where a ship bound for Livorno would be put at his disposal.

The Bingleys and Elizabeth were to remain in Aix for Easter, a time when the Provencals exchanged *les cloches de Paques,* the eggs that symbolized the risen Lord, with family and friends, and Charles was eager to attend a bullfight in Nîmes associated with the Feast of Pentecost.

Between the two holy days, there were goodbyes to be said. Cassie was particularly unhappy to leave Aix. In the months since their arrival, the little girl had become attached to Mademoiselle Marie, her nursemaid, as well as Monsieur and Madame Lavelle. Fortunately, news that Mr. Darcy had a daughter very near to her age had succeeded in restoring the child to her usual affability.

With Cassie by her side, Elizabeth returned to the town square as she had her own goodbyes to make. While sitting at an outdoor table with the sun on their faces, Elizabeth and Cassie enjoyed the local seed sable biscuits one last time before taking their leave of Madame.

Like her young charge, Elizabeth was reluctant to leave Aix. There were many reasons for her hesitation, none greater than her apprehension at seeing Mr. Darcy. But there were also advantages. As Charles's sister-in-law, she would be able to enjoy Mr. Darcy's company without inviting comment. She only hoped that the man's talents as a conversationalist had improved.

When the date for their departure arrived, Elizabeth and Cassie were the first to board the ship. From the vantage point of the ship's deck, aunt and niece were able to observe the beehive of activity that was the port of Marseille. With all manner of dress on display and a dozen languages being spoken, all at the same time, everything appeared higgledy-piggledly. Despite the confusion on the docks, there was a constant movement of ships in and out of the port.

When Mr. and Mrs. Bingley finally boarded the ship, they were in the company of Mr. Ned Farrow, the Bingley's shipping agent, a man whose position with the firm required that he sail back and forth between Marseille and Livorno and to nowhere else.

"I've been working at the Livorno warehouse since 1786 when it was opened by your father and his brother, Mr. George Bingley the Elder, that were," the agent said, addressing Charles. "The Farrow family knew the Bingleys from their time together in Scarborough, and your father and uncle took me on when I was a little older than your little girl," Farrow said, pointing to Cassie. "Well, that might be an exaggeration, but you take my meaning, sir. I were a lad. When England was fighting the Frogs, your father sent me to India, but I've been in Livorno since '17, four years now."

Canvassing the ship, Charles indicated that the crew looked a "rather rough lot."

"...and in need of a wash," Jane added.

"You might find this hard to believe, Mrs. Bingley, but my crew is Sunday clean when compared to some men I've been out to sea with. For many sailing men, the last time they had anything but rainwater poured over their heads was when they was in church being christened," a statement that caused Farrow to burst into guffaws.

While looking at the layered filth of the crew, Jane stated her own opinion. "I agree, Mr. Farrow. I would find that difficult to believe."

At Jane's remark, Elizabeth snickered. From the time she was a little girl, the eldest Bennet had been the prissy sister. Each birthday, Jane was given gifts of scented soap and toilet water. In England, whenever she was in London, she always carried a perfumed handkerchief wherever she went. In France, she had taken to carrying a bouquet of posies.

With night approaching, having accepted the captain's generous offer to use his private quarters as their berth, the party went below deck, hoping that with a good wind and calm seas, they would soon be in view of the Italian mainland.

* * *

Unfortunately, the wind was too good and the seas anything but calm. As a result, they were unable to venture up on deck, thus becoming prisoners of the weather. Although Cassie fared well enough, for the adults, the voyage proved to be the longest days of their lives. On the third day, with great relief, Charles opened the door to Mr. Farrow's knock. The agent came bearing the welcomed news that Leghorn was now in view, and their misery was nearing an end.

After putting Cassie's hair in the ringlets she so loved and checking on Jane, who lay across the captain's bed with arms splayed, Elizabeth saw to her toilette. Looking in the small beveled mirror, she winced at her reflection. With the extreme humidity of the Mediterranean, there was no help for her hair. In an attempt to bring color to her ashen face, she pinched her cheeks and bit her lips, but her efforts only served to accentuate how pale she was.

"Well, Cassie, there is no hope for improvement," Elizabeth said to the red-headed bundle watching her. "Even though I look a fright, there is no one in Leghorn who knows me, so I am safe from the criticisms of others."

After doing the best she could with her hair, Elizabeth offered to help Jane with hers. The eldest Bennet daughter, with her fair skin and blonde hair, looked even worse than her sister, and so Elizabeth suggested they go up on deck and breathe in the fresh air. Once on deck, the sunshine and breezes proved a palliative. From their perch, they were given a grand view of the port of Livorno and Fortezza Vecchia, the extensive red-stone harbor fortifications built by the Renaissance Medicis.

During the night, the seas had calmed, and their transfer to a rowboat went much smoother than it had at Dieppe, but just as costly, as open palms greeted their every movement. Knowing their journey was to end shortly, Elizabeth already felt better, and when Charles assisted her out of the boat, better still.

As soon as the Bingley party was on the pier, they were approached by a man who identified himself as Porter Eldridge, a portly man who would do well to push away from the supper table sooner rather than later and to avoid the pudding altogether.

"I knew your father, Mr. Bingley Sr.," Mr. Eldridge said by way of introduction. "A good man with a head for business. When he saw the French were to be our enemies, he hired a Greek to run the enterprise. As a result, Monsieur Napoleon left us alone. Once the Royal Navy bottled him up on that God-forsaken island, the English were back again making profits," he said, practically licking his lips. "He's dead, you know."

"Who is dead?" Jane asked.

"Napoleon. Died five days ago, on May 5, he did. Only just getting the news."

Elizabeth and the Bingleys exchanged looks. Whilst in Aix, they were aware that Napoleon's health was failing, but because the man had embroiled Europe in war for most of their lives, it was difficult to think of this giant of history as being no more. Although no Englishman would shed a tear at his passing, that was not true of his countrymen. Despite the heartache he had brought to France with the loss of so many of their young men, he remained a hero to the French, and they knew the people of Aix would grieve his loss.

"I hear they buried him in four coffins, one inside the next, which is four too many for my purposes. The soldiers who were guarding him should have thrown him in the ground with some quicklime," Eldridge added. "I have nothing good to say about the man. Lost a nephew in the Peninsular campaign."

Pointing to a four-story warehouse, which he identified as belonging to the Bingley family, Mr. Eldridge indicated that its contents were barrels of wheat from the Black Sea. After transferring its contents to English "bottoms" anchored in Leghorn, the grain was destined for British ports.

Charles, who, by preference, remained ignorant of the operations of the firm that made him rich, listened to stories of the trade transacted under the supervision of his cousin, George Bingley the Younger, who, Charles was pleased to learn, was not in Livorno. If the man's conversation was as obtuse as his annual reports, Charles was happy to be spared his company.

On the way to Eldridge's townhouse, the party drove through the heart of Livorno and the Piazza Grande, passing the Palace of the Governor and the Duomo. During the carriage ride, Elizabeth admired the yellow and rust colors of the townhouses, their red-tile roofs glowing in the late afternoon sun. She also noted the energy of the town, with men dressed in the clothes of a laborer, as well as English businessmen, hurrying every which way. Mr. Eldridge, serving as their guide, explained that the residents of Livorno slept during the heat of the day, only to awaken in late afternoon with the renewed vigor she was witnessing. Despite her reluctance to visit the Italian peninsula, her first impressions were all good.

When they arrived at Eldridge's townhouse, a five-story, yellow-stucco building with a commanding view of the harbor and Ligurian Sea, their host explained that the building was as much hotel as private home.

"When anyone comes to Leghorn from England or is on their way home to England, I must put them up, and I am happy to do it. In that way, I have first-hand news of what is happening in England and Alexandria and every place in between. But right now, me and Mrs. Eldridge have only the one guest besides yourselves, and there's room enough for all."

Similar in layout to the townhouses of London, the ground floor was merely an entryway, whose purpose was to separate the family from the dust, dirt, and noise of the street, and the guests were immediately led upstairs to the private rooms.

"I'm sure the missus is out on the balcony," Eldridge said, and in short quick steps, he led the way. "Yes, here she is as well as our visitor, Mr. Darcy of Derbyshire, who, I understand, is known to you all."

Although Jane bowed her head in acknowledgment and Charles quickly approached his friend to shake his hand, Elizabeth remained rooted to the spot, as immobile as the red terrazzo tiles beneath her.

"Miss Elizabeth, it has been too long," Darcy said, extending his hand, but a stunned Elizabeth did not take it.

"Aunt Elizabeth, Mr. Darcy wishes to take your hand," little Cassie squeaked.

"If that is agreeable, Miss Elizabeth, I do wish to take your hand."

Without thinking, she removed her glove and slowly lifted the hand that had been pinned to her side. Looking into Mr. Darcy's gray-green eyes, Elizabeth offered it to the gentleman, and when he accepted it, she knew she was in trouble.

Chapter 7

Between Charles's effusive greeting of his friend and the gentleman's attention to Cassie Bingley, Elizabeth's considerable discomposure went unnoticed. Despite the distractions, Elizabeth wanted to hide. She did not need a mirror to see that she looked like something the cat had dragged in.

If I had known Mr. Darcy was to be in Livorno, I would have taken more care with my appearance. And what on earth is he doing here? He is supposed to be in Florence. Obviously, he is not in Florence because he is standing not three feet away from me talking to Cassie. With my hair so blowsy, I shall make a very poor impression on the gentleman. Oh bother! What does it matter? Mr. Darcy is not interested in me.

"Do I have the honor of addressing Miss Cassandra Bingley?" Darcy asked the little girl.

As her aunt had done, Cassie nodded and held out her hand, and Darcy took it, giving it a gentle squeeze.

"Last time I saw you, Miss Bingley, you were in your cradle. You are a little taller now."

Cassie rewarded Darcy's comment with a smile. "Mama told me you have a little girl. Is she here?"

"Yes, my daughter is upstairs having a nap or *siesta* as it is called here in Livorno, but she will join us for supper."

"What is her name?"

"Alexandra, but I call her Alexa, and she is just a little older than you."

Cassie would not have to wait for supper, as a bouncing bundle of blonde curls, and one who was missing her two front teeth, burst onto the balcony, and Elizabeth had her first look at Mr. Darcy's daughter, who greatly resembled her mother. After circling the group of visitors, she immediately went to her father's side and slipped her small hand into his.

Beginning with Mr. and Mrs. Bingley, Darcy introduced Alexa to their company. With a perfect curtsey, she greeted each one. It was soon apparent that her interest was not in the grown-ups, but Cassie. In her eagerness to be with someone closer to her own age, she ignored the adults and informed her father that she was taking her new friend to her room.

Addressing Jane, Mr. Darcy apologized for his daughter. "Because Alexa has been so eager to have a playmate, she is forgetting her manners. That is one explanation. The other is that we have been without a governess for the past four months, and her nursery maid seems incapable of telling my daughter she cannot do something."

"You need a good English governess," Jane offered.

"I agree, and I sent to England for one, Mrs. Bingley. Upon her arrival, Miss Constance Plumber of Winchester was surprised to learn that Florentines do not speak English! She insisted that she had credible information indicating that most of Florence was made up of God-fearing Protestant Englishmen. I am sure she was referring to a well-established English colony in the city, a group of dedicated fans of Florence who call the city home. When Miss Plumber realized that was not the case, she insisted I make arrangements for her to return home! If only she had thought to ask *me*, her employer, about the occupants of the city, she would not have had to come so far."

Mr. Darcy then inquired after the Bennet family, and Jane assured the gentleman that everyone at Longbourn and in Meryton was in good health. She thought it best to say nothing of Lydia.

While Jane and Mr. Darcy conversed, Elizabeth thought how ill advised it had been for her to agree to go to Florence. What must he be thinking!

He is thinking that if I am to have the pleasure of Mr. Bingley's company, then I must take the good with the bad. But his manners are so pleasant and his words spoken with such civility.

Mr. Eldridge, who had remained silent while old friends renewed acquaintances, indicated that there was no reason to stand on the balcony overlooking the gardens. Instead, he would arrange for tea to be served *in* the gardens.

Like the townhouses of Paris, behind the plain facades and shuttered windows were elegant, high-ceilinged apartments with luxurious gardens on view from multiple balconies embracing a courtyard. With spring edging closer to summer, the visitors were treated to a rich palette of colors.

As Charles was eager to hear all about the upcoming Palio, Elizabeth was spared the necessity of conversing, which was a good thing, because her thoughts were a muddle. Amazed at her own discomposure, she was feeling very much like Lydia and Kitty while in the presence of a handsome officer wearing his regimentals.

"All in good time, Bingley," Darcy said to his overly eager friend. "You have been in Tuscany for less than a day."

"My husband has greatly missed your companionship," Jane interjected. "Charles was hoping to ride and shoot once we are in Florence."

"And so we shall. It is already arranged."

"And the spa at Bagno Vignoni?" Jane asked, her raised voice indicating her interest in that particular subject. "Is it very far from Florence?"

Darcy explained that the spa was a full day's ride from the city center. With its location in a rural area, the roads were poorly maintained, but he insisted it was well worth the trouble.

"Have you been there yourself, Mr. Darcy?" Jane asked.

"Yes, I have been twice as my late wife enjoyed the spa's regimen."

Although Jane had written to Mr. Darcy at the time of his wife's death, this was the first time she had been in the man's company since that sad event. "Mr. Darcy, I am so sorry for your loss."

"I thank you for your condolences, Mrs. Bingley. In fact, it is Amelie who brings me to Livorno as she is interred here in the Protestant cemetery, and yesterday Alexa and I visited her tomb. I do what I can to remind my daughter that her mother was once a daily presence in her life."

At that point, Mrs. Eldridge suggested the ladies might wish to freshen up, and they agreed to meet in a half hour for tea in the garden. Once in the room she was to share with Cassie Bingley, Elizabeth plunged her hands into the cool water of the basin and washed her face. Looking in the mirror, she wondered if there was ever a time when she had looked worse than she did at that moment. Her conclusion was that two winters ago, when she had suffered a bout of influenza, she had looked worse. *But not by much.*

After pulling the pins out of her hair, Elizabeth brushed it, but once again, the humidity worked against her. Finally, she twisted her hair and put in enough pins to keep it in place. Deciding that she had done her best, she sat down on the bed, and her thoughts turned to Mr.

Darcy. His time in Tuscany had been good to him. He was fit and tan and as tall and handsome as ever. Although there was now gray at the temples, it only served to accentuate his beautiful dark hair and gray-green eyes. His good looks were enough to make a girl go weak at the knees, but then she was no longer a girl. Instead, the woman in the mirror was now seven and twenty. Her time to attract a gentleman like Mr. Darcy had passed.

When Jane and Elizabeth rejoined the gentlemen, the pair was discussing the journey from Marseille to Livorno.

"To be perfectly honest, Darcy, it was damned awful," Charles said.

"I can certainly believe it," Darcy said, nodding in agreement, "but the roads between Aix and the Italian frontier are rugged in the extreme. I can almost guarantee that you would not have reached your destination without having to replace an axle, that is, if you could find someone with the skill necessary to replace it or, for that matter, the axle. There is also the matter of the most primitive accommodations you will find between Paris and Florence. You would not have wished to subject your wife, daughter, and sister-in-law to such conditions."

After the tea was served, Darcy asked the Bingleys and Elizabeth what they thought of Paris, and it was soon apparent that the interests of Charles and Jane Bingley were quite different from those of Elizabeth Bennet.

"Whilst my lady's maid and I went in one direction," Jane explained, "Lizzy and Cassie went in another."

"You travel with a lady's maid?" Mrs. Eldridge asked, looking around as if the maid might be hiding behind a chair.

"My maid was with me until Vichy. When she refused to go any farther from England, we had to send her home. Elizabeth has taken her place, but please do not judge her skills by how I look today. After such a voyage, even the best lady's maid could not have done better."

The news that Mrs. Bingley regarded her sister as her lady's maid caused Darcy to look at Elizabeth, and she met his gaze. The reality of her situation was that she was entirely dependent upon the Bingleys. It could not be kept a secret.

"And you, Miss Elizabeth, I gather you preferred the Louvre," Darcy said, rescuing her from further embarrassment. "Well, we must give credit where credit is due. Napoleon stole only the very best. Since I was last at the Musée du Louvre, I understand the collection has been expanded to include Egyptian antiquities."

Elizabeth indicated that his intelligence was accurate, but confessed her interest was more in the realm of fine arts than in mummies and sarcophagi.

"If that is the case, then you will love Florence."

"Yes, I am eagerly looking forward to visiting the sights," Elizabeth said, rising, "but if you will excuse me, I want to see what Cassie is doing."

"I can tell you what Cassie is doing," Darcy answered. "She is enjoying tea with my daughter and the nursery maid."

"Lizzy is the doting aunt," Jane said. "She and Cassie are nearly inseparable."

"I can easily believe it," Darcy answered. "However, in this case, the novelty of having a new friend will triumph over the familiar. Please sit down, Miss Elizabeth. I am curious to learn what you thought of Aix."

You do me no favor, Mr. Darcy, by keeping me here. Even so, Elizabeth did as the gentleman requested.

* * *

It was anticipated that the party would depart Livorno in three days' time. By then, the Bingley carriage would be reassembled and at their disposal. At supper, there were discussions about what the tourists should do during their stay in the Tuscan port city. The Eldridges offered several suggestions, but there was little enthusiasm on the part of the Bingleys for seeing the local sights, especially when the Duomo was mentioned. Jane declared that she had visited enough churches in Paris alone to last her a lifetime.

"I can understand your fatigue, Mrs. Bingley, with the Gothic and Romanesque churches in France," Darcy said, "but it is quite different here in Italy. You never know when you may stumble into a church and find yourself admiring a fresco by Giotto or looking at a sculpture by Michelangelo. In Rome, I sheltered in a church during a rainstorm and passed the time by admiring three epic works by Caravaggio."

"If you wish to speak of art, sir, you would do best to address my sister," Jane answered. "We had no sooner set foot on French soil, then Lizzy was keen to visit the local sites. On the road from Dieppe to Paris, we were required to spend a full day visiting the cathedral at Rouen. Whilst in Paris, she made arrangements to visit St. Denis with a group of fellow Englishmen, and then there was that little church in..."

Although her words indicated annoyance, Jane's tone betrayed their true intent. Even though she did not share her sister's interests in the arts and fine buildings, Jane had ensured that resources were made available so that Elizabeth could see everything she wished to see, including a visit to Versailles, a palace ignored by the current monarch in favor of the Tuileries.

"As I have an interest in architecture, I would be found guilty of the same charge, but your interest is in spas. May I ask what your impression of Vichy was?" Darcy asked changing the subject to one that would be of interest to Mrs. Bingley. "It is one of the few spas in France that my wife and I did not visit."

"I was told that because Napoleon's mother enjoyed the spa that vast improvements were made, including the building of hydrotherapeutic facilities, and improvements will continue because the Duchess of

Angouleme has taken an interest. She is the daughter of Marie Antoinette and Louis XVI and a great favorite of the French people. She was in residence while we there. Wherever she goes, a crowd gathers."

"Odd thing that," Charles said. "I understand that royalty is to be treated with deference, but it was as if this woman were a saint with a line of silent pilgrims walking behind her."

"Considering that her parents were executed on the orders of an illegitimate government, and only God knows what happened to her brother, the French probably view her survival as nothing short of a miracle," Darcy offered. "But Mrs. Bingley was speaking of the spa at Vichy."

Discussing spas was one of Jane's favorite topics. In her search for a cure for the ailments that inhibited her return to robust health, she sought out those who had visited the various European spas. And it was not just the physical that was of concern, but a lack of clarity in her thinking that her physician described as mental confusion. Before Cassie's birth, Jane would never have described Elizabeth as being her lady's maid. But there were signs that better days were coming. While in Vichy, and again in Aix, Jane had mentioned that the incessant tingling she experienced in her feet following Cassie's birth had ceased. Of equal importance was improvement in Jane's mental acuity. The forgetfulness that had plagued her was dissipating.

"If I understand you correctly, Mrs. Bingley, you are not interested in seeing the sights of Livorno, but your sister is." Jane nodded. "In that case, Miss Elizabeth, would you allow me to show you points of interest in the town?"

"That is very kind of you, Mr. Darcy, and I accept your generous offer," Elizabeth quickly answered. "Cassie will be pleased. She is so very curious."

"Lizzy, I did not mean for you to take Cassie," Jane said, interrupting. "She will be content to remain here with Miss Darcy."

At the suggestion that Mr. Darcy and she would ride around Livorno unchaperoned, Elizabeth went wide eyed, and by her expression, Jane understood her objection.

"Lizzy, this is not England. There is no one here to criticize, and Mr. Darcy is a family friend."

"I would ask that you consider my offer, Miss Elizabeth, as you would be doing me a favor. Since my wife's death, Alexa has been my constant companion. If we are parted for only a few hours, she becomes anxious. I think Cassie will prove to be an excellent diversion for her. Besides, we shall not be gone all that long. Livorno is not exactly Florence."

With all eyes upon her, Elizabeth felt she had no choice but to agree. Although she gave no hint of it, she was pleased with the idea of being shown about town by none other than Fitzwilliam Darcy of Pemberley.

Chapter 8

As agreed, Elizabeth waited in the garden for Mr. Darcy to begin their tour of Livorno, but he was late—very late—and she could guess the reason for his tardiness. The previous evening, when Mr. Darcy had mentioned the outing, Alexa had suggested that they should *all* go on a picnic in one of Livorno's many parks. Although her father had stated that she would remain with Mr. and Mrs. Bingley and enjoy the company of her new friend, it appeared that, in private, the little girl had won the argument.

A disappointed Elizabeth was gathering her belongings when Mr. Darcy burst into the garden. With the expectation of seeing Alexa trailing behind, she looked passed the gentleman, but found he was alone.

"Miss Elizabeth, my apologies. I was delayed. Obviously, I was delayed. But I am here now. Shall we?" he said, gesturing toward the door, and Elizabeth asked where they were going.

"Excellent question," he said, clearly flustered. "Do you wish to see the Duomo?"

"Is it worth seeing?" Elizabeth asked and then added a smile to put the man at his ease.

"Not really. Compared to Notre Dame and Sainte Chapelle, it is nothing."

From his unsettled look, Elizabeth could see that he had given no thought to their tour. Trying to be helpful, Elizabeth asked if it were possible to drive around the town. Darcy nodded, and in fluent Italian, gave directions to the driver.

The carriage headed toward the Venetian district, so named because of its many bridges and canals. Along its pathways and on its bridges, sellers hawked their wares. With mid-day approaching, vendors were out in front of their shops encouraging passersby to come in and enjoy a *torta de ceci* made with chickpeas.

From the district, they drove along a road paralleling the sea, the perfect route in which to admire the Tuscan coast. While viewing the considerable fortifications built by the Medicis, they enjoyed a fish stew at a small cafe. Although the *cacciucco* was very good, it was the view of the harbor that gave Elizabeth the most pleasure, and with the heat of the day upon them, they benefitted from a strong breeze bringing along with it the smell of the sea.

When they returned to the carriage, Darcy gave the driver specific instructions as to the next segment of their tour. After climbing a rather steep hill, they arrived at a statue honoring Ferdinando I of the House of Medici. At its base were four sculptures of Spanish

Moors in chains with the faces of the prisoners ranging from despair to agony. Perched on its pedestal, the figure of the Grand Duke of Tuscany stared out unto the Ligurian Sea, oblivious to the suffering of the prisoners at his feet.

"So Ferdinando fought the Moors?" Lizzy asked.

"I believe he fought the Turks," Darcy answered, and then made a face as if chewing on that bit of history. "In truth, I have no idea what inspired this statue," he said, throwing up his arms, "but don't you think it serves as an excellent conversational piece?"

"It certainly does." Both started to laugh at their ignorance.

"Shall we walk, Miss Elizabeth?" Darcy asked, offering his arm.

Elizabeth slipped her arm into his, and in her imagination, she envisioned the pair walking, not in Livorno, but through Pemberley's extensive gardens as man and wife. In her role as mistress of the manor, she would make suggestions for improvements to the grounds, possibly the addition of a maze for the amusement of their many guests, but these pleasant thoughts were interrupted by Mr. Darcy who felt he owed her an explanation for his tardiness. As suspected, the reason was Alexa.

"Since my wife's death, with few exceptions, Alexa has been by my side. I thought, with the passage of time, that would change, but it has not. Part of the difficulty is that I have been unable to keep a governess.

I told you about the English lady, but there were others as well: two French and one Italian. One of the French ladies was too strict—Alexa could do no right—while the other spent her day eating sweets. And, my goodness, the Florentine! Alexa could have burnt down the house, and the woman would have found reason to admire her work. At present, Flora, the daughter of my housekeeper, has taken on the role, but this cannot continue. Something must be done."

Elizabeth agreed, but that *something* must start with her father.

"Why are you smiling, Miss Elizabeth?"

"Alexa is an intelligent child and takes her cues from you."

"Can you be more specific?"

"Last night, when you told Alexa it was time for her to go to bed, she succeeded in extending her play time with Cassie for another thirty minutes. And why should she not? If my father looked at me in the same way as you look at your daughter, I would know that I had won the argument."

"But there is a reason why she acts as she does. You see, my daughter is frightened. She believes that if we are not always together that I shall leave her."

"Because of her mother's death?"

Darcy nodded. He explained that every morning, Alexa and her mother would start the day with a story that Amelie would read to the child in bed.

"Of course, the day came when she could not join her mother. How do you explain death to a five-year-old?" Darcy asked with a profound sadness in his voice.

"Mr. Darcy, I am very sorry for your loss. I was only in Mrs. Darcy's company on a few occasions, but she appeared to be perfectly amiable and was most definitely beautiful."

"Thank you for that. But does it help to explain my difficulties with Alexa?"

"Yes, it does, and a possible solution to your problem may be at hand." A hopeful Darcy waited for Elizabeth to continue. "Cassie Bingley is a delightful child, and I think in the very near future you will find Alexa prefers Cassie's company to yours."

From Mr. Darcy's look, it was evident that Elizabeth's answer did not satisfy—that he had anticipated a different response—leaving her to wonder what he thought she was going to say.

* * *

As soon as Elizabeth was in her room, there was a knock on the door, and she knew exactly who had come calling.

"Well?" Jane asked.

"Well, I had a very nice day, but I did not see the Duomo."

"Oh, who cares about an old church?" Jane said, laughing. "I was expecting you in the early afternoon and then late afternoon, and here it is evening. You will barely have enough time to change for supper."

"If you must know, we drove up to Monte Nero where there is a basilica dedicated to Our Lady of Grace. Over the main altar, there is an icon of the Virgin that is lavishly decorated with marble cherubs and golden sunbursts."

"Lizzy, you are teasing me. You know what I want to hear. How did you and Mr. Darcy get on?"

"Fine. We got on fine. During my tour of the city and its surroundings, the gentleman shared with me everything he knew about Livorno, and then we came back here."

"Really?" Jane said with a squinty-eyed look. "All you talked about was Livorno?"

"Actually, no," Elizabeth said, sitting down on the settee. "Mr. Darcy spoke of his wife. In every gesture and statement, it was evident how much he loves and misses her. I know what you want to hear—that Mr. Darcy has some interest in me—but that is not the case. It was as if he and I had no shared past. It was all about Mrs. Darcy and their daughter."

"That really is too bad. I was hoping he would make you another offer."

"You cannot be serious!" Elizabeth said, laughing, and then she pointed to the door. "Out! I must see to my toilette before supper, and I cannot do that if I am laughing at your comments concerning Mr. Darcy."

After her sister left, her words resonated. "Marry Mr. Darcy? I wish it were so," Elizabeth said to an empty room.

Chapter 9

After supper, while Mr. and Mrs. Eldridge and Mr. and Mrs. Bingley played cards and the two girls played jacks on the uneven tiles of the terrazzo, Elizabeth begged an audience with Mr. Darcy as she had thought of an idea that might help the gentleman with his daughter.

'Do you have affairs to attend to in Livorno, Mr. Darcy?"

"I do."

"While you go about your business, is it your intention to bring your daughter along?" Elizabeth could tell by his expression that he had. "May I suggest you leave Alexa with me?"

"Actually, that is not necessary. When I need to pay calls, Alexa is no problem at all as she entertains herself with her sketchbook."

"By that statement, I take it to mean that either you want Alexa to accompany you or that you have no wish to address the problem we discussed at this time."

Darcy pursed his lips, but Elizabeth decided that the gentleman's annoyance was a result of her getting it right.

"Alexa would be very unhappy if I were to leave her two days in a row. She would cry."

"Children often cry, Mr. Darcy. It is what they do, and if it gets them what they want, they continue to cry for the simple reason that it works to their benefit."

"Yes, of course," he said, acknowledging the obvious. "After we retire, I shall discuss it with Alexa."

"Please excuse my interference, but I do not think that is the best way to go about it. I would suggest you say nothing to Alexa. In the morning, after breakfast, tell her you have business in the city and leave—just go. It is the best way."

"You are offering these suggestions based on your experience with Cassie, but Cassie did not lose her mother."

"I mean no disrespect, Mr. Darcy, but this afternoon, you asked what was to be done about Alexa. My suggestions would make for a good start." Darcy looked skeptical. "You should do this, not just for your daughter, but for yourself. You must have a life apart from your child. It is more than a year since your wife's passing. It is time."

For a few minutes, Darcy sat in silence with his eyes closed, and Elizabeth thought he was angry with her. But after digesting what she had said, he began to nod.

"Yes, I *do* need to establish a life apart from Alexa, and as you said, the time has come and not just for the reasons mentioned. You see, it is my intention to return to England, that is, after Bingley has seen the Palio and Mrs. Bingley has enjoyed the waters at Bagno Vignoni, so that I might resume some semblance of a social life."

Darcy explained that following his wife's death, it had not been his intention to remain in Tuscany for so long, but because his daughter drew comfort from the familiar surroundings, he had stayed.

"But I now realize we have stayed too long. My daughter does not think of herself as English. And why should she?" Darcy asked. "She lives in Florence, and her friends, the children of the servants, are all Florentines. Occasionally, we visit with the families of the English community, but there are few children amongst that group and none as young as she. And I must look to the future. I can hardly believe Alexa is already six years old. Before you know it, it will be her time to come out into society, and that cannot happen in Florence. She is English and must marry an Englishman.

"There is another consideration," Darcy added. "I find life in Florence to be limiting."

"Really? Why is that?"

"Because it is a society unwelcoming of strangers. Of course, there are exceptions, my neighbor Count Roberto Bardi, for example, but by and large, the social life of the English revolves around the British Consul. It is through him that all things are possible. As a result, I move in a confined, unvarying society."

Mr. Darcy provided an example. Above the streets of Florence, an elevated walkway connected the Palazzo Vecchio with the Palazzo Pitti across the Arno River. The Medici rulers had used the walkway as a means of avoiding contact with the people on the street below. However, the walkway was no drab passageway, but a corridor lined with portraits of the Medicis painted by the Old Masters. Private access to Florence's celebrated Uffizi Gallery was through a doorway from the hidden walkway.

"Anyone who is properly attired may visit the Uffizi, but in order to view the paintings in the private corridor, one must receive an invitation issued at the request of the British Consul. I have a standing request with Sir Martin Spencer, but as of this date, he has been unable to secure the necessary pass. As the great Florentine families go north toward the Italian Alps for the summer, it should not be a problem, but they deny access because it is a way for them to exercise what little power remains to them."

"Considering how insular the English are, it seems only fair that we be treated as we treat others."

"Yes, we dish it out at home and must sample it abroad," Darcy said, nodding in agreement. "But I would like you to know that I have again written to the Consul asking that he secure the necessary passes. One can hope."

Elizabeth smiled in such a way that it prompted Mr. Darcy to ask the reason. He was pleased that he had amused her, but he must know why.

"You are not used to being told 'no,'" Lizzy said, smiling. "It irks you to be denied an invitation that you covet."

Darcy laughed. Her response reminded him of their time together at Netherfield Park. She had declared to Caroline Bingley that the easiest way to punish him for a remark he had made was to tease him—to laugh at him—which was exactly what she was doing now. She had taken his measure early on, but what she did not know was that life had changed him. He was a different man from the one who had engaged her in such repartee in Netherfield's drawing room.

"It is true that being denied admittance to the Vasari Corridor *irks* me, as you say. However, I was never invited to Almack's nor to the king's levees, and I bore it with grace," he answered, "but great art belongs to the world and should not be hidden away."

"Be careful, Mr. Darcy, or you will be accused of having revolutionary ideas and may find yourself in trouble with your Tory friends."

"If you must know, I am a supporter of most Whig policies."

Now it was Elizabeth's turn to be surprised. "My goodness, Mr. Darcy! I had no idea. The owner of a great and ancient estate and the grandson of an earl, a Whig? You are a contradiction, sir."

"I have been called worse."

"As I am the daughter of a Tory, we had best steer clear of politics and return to the neutral topic of art. Seeing the Corridor would be nice, but I foresee no difficulty in filling my time whilst in Florence."

"I do not think a lifetime is sufficient to see all that Florence has to offer."

"But to return to our conversation regarding Alexa," Elizabeth said while looking at Mr. Darcy's little girl, who was now playing draughts with Cassie. It was clear from the arrangement of the board that the pair had made up their own rules. "If it is your intention to return to England in the near future, then it is even more important that you leave the child with me. Once you are at Pemberley, it will be necessary for you to employ a governess because, if you do not, your daughter will not receive the proper education necessary for a young lady of rank. If you would allow me to act in that capacity during our time in Florence, it may make it much easier for you when you return home."

"A governess! Miss Elizabeth, I can assure you that it would be impossible for me to look upon you as a governess. I am a gentleman, and you are gentleman's daughter. As such, we are equal."

"I appreciate that, Mr. Darcy," Lizzy said, surprised to learn that Mr. Darcy considered her his equal. That certainly had not been his opinion when they were together in Kent. "In this case, 'governess' is merely a term of convenience. I have offered to oversee Cassie's lessons. Why should your daughter not be included? After all, you have been gracious enough to invite me into your home. By helping with Alexa, I am provided with an opportunity to repay your kindness. Once you are in England, you will want to find a properly trained governess to see to Alexa's lessons."

"Everything you say is true, but I am dreading looking for another governess. I am just not very good at it."

"Perhaps your sister will be able to assist you in that regard."

"Yes, I have written to Georgiana seeking her help, but she already has her hands full."

Darcy explained that his sister had married Mr. Christopher Legh, a cousin of Baron Newtown of Lyme Park, a widower with three young children. Although Legh had an estate of his own in Cheshire, he had agreed to live at Pemberley until such time as its master returned to Derbyshire.

"Christopher and Georgiana have two of their own children with a third on the way. When I last visited Pemberley, the house was in an uproar. There was a child behind every door and under every table. It is a joyful place and a pleasure to be in their company."

"Although I never met your sister, I have heard only good reports of her kindness and amiability. I am pleased to hear she is happily married and living in a place so dear to her heart."

"And mine as well," Darcy said, nodding. "I much prefer the country to town. It was not always thus, but after several weeks of forced cheerfulness, banal conversation, and excessive eating during the London season, I long for the solitude of Pemberley. That is where I am happiest. As I have already mentioned, I never meant to stay away for so long, but Alexa was so affected by her mother's death that I thought it best not to unsettle her further."

"I am sure you have chosen wisely, but once Alexa is at Pemberley, I am equally sure she will be happy." Elizabeth confessed that she had visited the estate with her Aunt and Uncle Gardiner. "We were on our way to Matlock, but being so near to a place I had heard so much about, I could not resist visiting."

"Did you tour the manor house?"

"We did not as the family was in residence, but we did meet your housekeeper. I believe her name is Mrs. Reynolds." Darcy nodded. "Before introducing us to the gardener, she was kind enough to give us a brief history of the house and the family."

"Did she mention me?"

"She did."

"And what did she say?"

"You will be happy to hear that your housekeeper was all praise for her master. She came very close to saying that you walked on water. Since we are in a country populated with adherents of the Roman faith, a better analogy might be that you would be a candidate for canonization."

Darcy burst out laughing at Elizabeth's exaggerated praise. "Before leaving for the Continent, I left Mrs. Reynolds with a script that she might use when speaking with visitors to the manor. From what you have said, I believe she was reading directly from my script," and he gave her a knowing smile. "So what did you think of Pemberley, Miss Elizabeth?"

"I have never seen a place for which nature has done more or where natural beauty has been so little counteracted by an awkward taste. The manor house is handsome, and your park is perfectly lovely."

"Thank you, Miss Elizabeth," Darcy said, nodding in agreement. "I can take little credit for the beauty of Pemberley. The original design was drawn up by my great grandfather and executed under the direction of my grandfather and father, and the interiors are a result of my mother's influence. My contribution is the Roman folly at the heart of the garden. It is modeled on Bramante's Tempietto. When I was a lad, I visited Rome with my father. Whilst there, I sketched the temple, and upon inheriting the estate, I began construction of the folly."

"Oh, the folly was my favorite place in the gardens!" Elizabeth exclaimed. "The view from there is magnificent."

"It is my favorite place as well," Darcy said, smiling.

"And what did Mrs. Darcy think of Pemberley?"

"Amelie liked it well enough, but she favored warmer climes."

That was to be the last word as it was time for Alexa and Cassie to go to bed. With Cassie holding her aunt's hand and Alexa clinging to her father, the four of them walked to their respective rooms. Before saying good night, Mr. Darcy agreed to Elizabeth's plan to leave his daughter behind while he saw to some business matters.

"I shall warn you, Miss Elizabeth, be prepared for tears."

"Oh, I am used to tears," Elizabeth answered. *I have shed enough of my own.*

Chapter 10

At breakfast, a teary-eyed Alexa made circles with her spoon in her porridge. There were two reasons for her unhappiness. Due to an early appointment, her father had decided not to eat breakfast with her. The second was that Miss Elizabeth was in charge until his return. Before she could protest, her father was gone.

Elizabeth was not unsympathetic. As imperfect as her own parents were, she was fortunate to have both a father and mother living. With the loss of her mother, it was only natural for Alexa to be apprehensive, but her unease should not translate into immobilizing her father. Surely, at some time in the future, Mr. Darcy would wish to remarry, and the daughter must make room for her stepmother.

To start off their new relationship, Elizabeth had declared the day to be lesson free, a decision that delighted Cassie but drew no response from Alexa. As it was Elizabeth's intention to fill the day with fun things to do, she felt that as the day progressed Mr. Darcy's daughter would become engaged.

Although not a portraitist, Elizabeth was capable of drawing a decent caricature, and she drew a sketch of Cassie riding a dolphin while skirting the waves beneath her. Her efforts managed to bring a smile to the face of the pouting Alexa, and she was promptly rewarded with her own sketch in which Alexa, with hands on the reins and hair flying, soared above the clouds on a goose. After taking the sketchbook from Elizabeth, Miss Darcy drew a picture of Elizabeth riding a pony backwards, her untethered curls flowing freely behind her. For so young a child, the sketch was quite good. With a competent drawing master, she might very well excel at drawing as Elizabeth had heard her mother had the same talent.

For their midday meal, the trio walked to the town center. With Alexa serving as their interpreter, Elizabeth treated the girls to *tortas de ceci* that were being sold from a cart in front of the Duomo. Although the dialect of Livorno was different from that of Florence, the child had no difficulty in making herself understood. Clearly, she was bright and intuitive. The right governess could easily make up for her neglected education.

An entirely perfect day was not to be expected. The first show of resistance to Elizabeth's authority came when they returned to the townhouse. When Elizabeth indicated that everyone must have an afternoon rest, Alexa declared that she did not need a siesta. Instead, she would read a book. Elizabeth agreed to the plan on the condition that Alexa must do her reading in her room with Cassie and whilst in bed. A brief skirmish ensued, but Elizabeth reminded her that her father had left her in charge and that her directions were orders, not suggestions. Within a half hour, both girls, with their hair cascading across their pillows, were sound asleep.

* * *

"How did it go with Miss Darcy?" Jane asked as she poured her sister a cup of tea.

"I think very well. Considering the child is used to having her own way, I thought she would put up more resistance. Like most children, she is in need of guidance. If Mr. Darcy hires a good governess, I think all will be well."

"Finding a good governess is a tall order. When you agreed to oversee Cassie's lessons, a burden was lifted off my shoulders," Jane said, reaching over to squeeze her sister's hand. "As you know, I had hoped to see to my daughter's lessons myself, but I have not the energy. Not yet. But I must admit I am feeling better. By the time we arrive back in England, I shall be as fit as a fiddle."

"I think you will," Elizabeth answered. "Your color has improved greatly, and I have noticed that you walk with more energy. As for your daughter, I love spending time with Cassie as she is as pleasant a child as can be. Knowing who her mother is, how could it be otherwise? I do not know of anyone with a more amiable disposition than Jane Bennet Bingley. During our childhood, I cannot remember either Mama or Papa scolding you at any time. I, on the other hand, was in constant need of correction."

"That is only because you were more adventuresome than I, and your curiosity has survived into adulthood. I still cannot believe you climbed to the very top of Notre Dame."

"For my efforts, I was richly rewarded. I had a bird's eye view of Paris and its bridges and great churches, the Palais Royal, and the whole of the Louvre. I would do it again in a heartbeat."

"Well, it is my understanding that Florence has a great many churches with a great many steps, and I am sure you will want to visit them all."

"I am not sure about all of them, but most definitely the Duomo. Now there is a challenge!"

After finishing her tea, Elizabeth placed the cup on the table and settled back into her chair. Although the day had been a carefree one, she was in need of her own siesta, but she fought off sleep as she did not want Mr. Darcy to return to find her sleeping.

"I am surprised Mr. Darcy has stayed away for so long," Elizabeth said, yawning. "I thought he would have rushed back here to make sure Alexa was not too unhappy with him."

"Oh, I forgot to tell you. Mr. Darcy *did* come back whilst you were upstairs with the girls. After I told him that all was well, he said he would take Mr. Eldridge up on his offer to view the Bingley operation in Livorno, and he dragged Charles along with him. My poor husband. He has no head for business, but he went anyway."

"Is Mr. Darcy to become a businessman?" Elizabeth asked. She could not imagine the Master of Pemberley reviewing account ledgers.

"According to Charles, Mr. Darcy already is," Jane said in a conspiratorial tone. "Apparently, he owns shares in Bingley enterprises here in Livorno and in England and India as well. It was a very smart move on his part to buy shares in commercial enterprises for what Charles's cousin, George Bingley, calls 'the realities of the post-war era,'" whatever that means."

Elizabeth was surprised to learn of Mr. Darcy's foray into the world of business, but she should not have been. When one thought of the depressed agricultural market, it made sense for Mr. Darcy to look for an income beyond farming. If only her father had done the same.

"Do you mind terribly, if I close my eyes?" Elizabeth asked.

"Your eyes are already closed."

"Then may I keep them closed?"

Elizabeth had no idea how much time had passed when she heard a voice declaring that "the children have exhausted Miss Elizabeth." Recognizing Mr. Darcy's baritone, she sat upright in her chair and found the gentleman staring at her.

"I was not asleep," she said, the thickness of her speech indicating otherwise. "I was just about to check on the children."

"Then let us go together."

When they entered the room, they found one of Mr. Eldridge's maids snoring in a chair, and the children, with their legs overlapping, sound asleep while sharing a pillow.

"As you can see, Mr. Darcy, your daughter survived your outing."

"Yes, she did," he said, admiring his offspring. "I am so grateful to you, Miss Elizabeth, for making it possible. Prior to today, the only times I went out without Alexa, it was late in the evening when she was already asleep. I must tell you I feel quite liberated. I went out, Alexa knew it, and the walls did not come tumbling down."

"It is my suggestion that you make a habit of it."

"And I shall. I have guests coming to stay at my villa in Florence, and I wish to be the best host possible," he said, referencing their upcoming journey. "And I have news about our departure. We have found excellent horses to pull Bingley's carriage, and so we shall leave as soon as we are packed. I am eager to show you—all of you—Florence."

"And I am eager to see it."

Chapter 11

Florence! After three days on the road, including two ferry crossings and stays at less than stellar accommodations, through the blue mist of a Tuscan sky, Elizabeth could make out the outline of a city in the distance. Within her view were beautiful villas dotting the hills above Florence, their acres covered with olive trees and grapevines and their fields plowed by the labors of yoked white oxen. As the carriage made its way across a bridge spanning the Arno, Elizabeth noted a series of other bridges, one supported by ornate Corinthian pillars, an indicator of Florence as the birthplace of Italy's classical revival, as well as the white sails of the boats traversing its waters.

Skirting the edge of the city, the carriage navigated narrow roads bordered by towering cypresses serving as elongated sentinels. The Darcy villa, Le Torri Dorate, sat at the end of a long drive lined with umbrella pines and populated by cats flitting in and out of the greenery. The palazzo, the color of ochre, was named for the tower that was attached to the west side of the villa and one that provided its residents with a view of the city below.

Alexa was eager to show her guests her favorite part of the villa—its gardens. With Cassie nipping at her heels, she marched her visitors through the entrance hall and drawing room and right out the French windows leading to a large terrace that provided a platform from which to view the glories of Le Torri Dorate. Unlike the gardens of England with their park-like settings, the layout was from an older era when formalized gardens, such as Elizabeth had seen at Versailles, were all the rage.

While Elizabeth and Jane walked the gravel path, the men remained on the terrace talking about the upcoming Palio in Pistoia, where the prize given to the winner was a valuable cloth banner or *palio*. When the ladies rejoined the men, Mr. Darcy suggested they might all enjoy a siesta, but Elizabeth shook her head. With eyes riveted on the tower, she indicated her preference.

"You are not overly fatigued from your journey, Miss Elizabeth?"

"No, sir, I am not as I was able to sleep in the carriage."

"Then you were the only one," he said. "Alexa talked all the way here. After I mentioned that you would be acting in the capacity of governess while you were at Le Torri Dorate, she posed one question after another."

"And her response to the news?"

"I will be honest with you. Alexa views you as a rival for my attention."

After turning the color of a Tuscan sunset, Elizabeth asked if he had corrected her.

"Actually, I told her that it was highly likely that during your stay, you would enjoy a good deal of my attention. After all, I am your host, and as such, it is my responsibility to ensure that your stay here in Florence is enjoyable. Shall we proceed?"

With narrow slits in the masonry providing glimpses of the surrounding countryside, Elizabeth climbed the nearly one-hundred steps to reach the top of the tower. After Mr. Darcy opened a wooden door groaning from age, she stepped out onto a small balcony that looked down on the heart of the city, a view dominated by the red tiles of Brunelleschi's dome.

"If you look to the left of the Duomo," Darcy said, "you will see the *campanile*, that is, the bell tower that dominates the Piazza della Signoria, the place of the rulers, the rulers, of course, being the Medicis."

As Mr. Darcy spoke, Elizabeth tried to absorb the information he was sharing, but with his arm brushing against her own, it was an impossible task made even more difficult by her imagining the Master of Pemberley slipping his arm around her waist and pulling her close to him. While glancing at his profile, she realized that if she removed her bonnet, she would fit perfectly under his chin.

"To the left of the campanile is the baptistery famous for Ghiberti and Pisano's bronze doors. Those three buildings represent birth, life, and death. We are baptized in the baptistery as infants, we celebrate the important rituals of our life in the Duomo, and the campanile points to heaven and our afterlife."

"One can hope that the campanile is pointing in the direction we are going," Elizabeth answered, finally finding her tongue.

With evening upon them, the rays of a setting sun were dancing on the roof of the Duomo, and Elizabeth had never seen anything so beautiful—not London—not Paris—but Firenze, the City of Flowers. With a vast Renaissance city sprawling below, it was difficult to take it all in, but during her sojourn, she would do her best to visit every site Mr. Darcy was describing.

"May we begin my tour of Florence with the history of this villa?"

"I am afraid it is a rather sad story, but I find that most tales that survive from generation to generation tend to be tragic. It seems people choose to jettison recollections of days of contentment and celebration in favor of those times when tragedy came knocking on their doors."

"Is the tragedy that knocked on the door of Le Torri Dorate from the distant past?"

"Yes. This particular tale comes to us from none other than Niccolo Machiavelli, the author of *The Prince*. His *Florentine Histories* is in the villa library in an English translation, and I encourage you to read it as it exposes all the machinations of Florence's most powerful families. Their constant feuding makes the War of the Roses look like a family quarrel. Do you still wish to hear it?"

"With such an introduction, how could I resist!"

"Within the walls of Le Torri Dorate lived Constanza Donati, the daughter of one of the most powerful families in Florence," Darcy began. "Although stories of her unparalleled beauty were known throughout Tuscany, no one outside her immediate family had ever actually seen her. However, the tale had reached the ears of the handsome, Angelo Buondelmonte. One evening, Buondelmonte climbed the walls surrounding the villa, and when he saw Constanza, he immediately fell in love with her. When he asked her father for her hand in marriage, Donati gave his consent. However, Buondelmonte neglected to inform Donati of one important detail: He was already engaged to a daughter of the house of Amidei.

"When news reached the Amidei and their allies, the Uberti, they swore revenge for the insult. The young man, who was unaware of the outrage his betrayal had aroused, was crossing a bridge over the Arno on Easter Sunday when he was set upon by members of the Uberti family, and he was slain near a statue of Mars, the God of War, thus beginning decades of war between the Buondelmontes and the Ubertis."

"Of all days to murder someone, the day we celebrate our risen Lord, the Prince of Peace!"

"As murderous thugs rarely go to church, they were available."

"What became of Constanza?" Lizzy said, laughing at his comment.

"According to legend, she retired to a convent, declaring that no man other than Angelo would ever know just how beautiful she was."

"I am pleased to hear that she did not take her life. This story bears a strong resemblance to *Romeo and Juliet*."

"In Italy, there are few love stories that do not. Murder, mayhem, internecine quarrels involving knives, swords, poison, all are grist for the storyteller, but then few love stories have happy endings."

"You mean few love stories *in literature* have happy endings," Elizabeth said, correcting him, "but then such tales are written for the purpose of tugging at one's heart strings."

Darcy laughed. "Your statement implies that in real life most love stories *do* have happy endings. I am sure you did not mean to say that, but if you did, I envy you your naiveté. But you were asking about the villa," he said, turning his back on the city. "For a brief time, Le Torri Dorate was also the home of the Countess of Albany, the wife of Bonnie Prince Charlie, who treated her very badly, and her *amour*, the poet, Count Vittorio Alfieri..." Darcy hesitated. "Is it permissible to mention such things?"

"Whilst in Tuscany, yes! But I might be of a different mind in England." Elizabeth could see a slight smile cross Mr. Darcy's face.

"After Alfieri's death, the countess erected a monument to her lover in Santa Croce."

"How romantic!"

"Yes, it is, but the monument is hideous. You may, however, decide for yourself as it is located between the monuments dedicated to Michelangelo and Machiavelli who are also buried in the basilica."

"Yes, I would very much like to see them." Elizabeth repeated her enthusiasm for viewing the treasures of the City of Flowers, but whilst listening to tales of Florence's past, she wondered about the man who was sharing its stories.

Chapter 12

After leaving the tower, Darcy and Elizabeth rejoined the Bingleys who were admiring the main hall of the villa that featured beautiful tiles of rust, green, gold, and black. The walls were painted a soft gold, and two large niches, displaying marble busts of ancient Romans, were painted a rich rust color. Inside the drawing room were floor-to-ceiling bookcases with their spines showing titles in Italian, German, and English, the floors were covered with thick Turkish carpets, and gossamer curtains were gathered in ornate clasps so that the breezes of this hilltop retreat could flow into the room.

While the guests were happily touring the villa and its gardens, the staff had prepared a sumptuous midday meal for Mr. Darcy's friends to be served in a dining room with a huge fresco depicting an olive grove with a palazzo in the distance. The china, a vibrant pattern of the Tuscan colors of rust and yellow, complemented the centerpiece, a pyramid of lemons. Lemons were everywhere: in the artwork, on the table, as garnish, and in their tea. Only the revered olive tree challenged its primacy. Everything connected with the villa spoke of wealth and leisure, a perfect retreat from the heat of summer as well as the heat of Florentine politics.

While dining, Elizabeth was teased by Charles, Jane, and Mr. Darcy for her childlike enthusiasm for visiting the sights. When one considered her pitiable finances, she had never thought to see Paris, but that had happened. Nor did she think she would visit the South of France, but for a few glorious months, she had called Aix-en-Provence home. And, now, here she was in Florence, the greatest city of the Renaissance.

Let them tease, she thought. *As long as I get to see Michelangelo's David and Ghiberti's bronze doors, I shall have the last laugh.*

Jane and Charles had already indicated that they would not be going into Florence until Jane had had a few days' rest. Since leaving Aix, Mrs. Bingley had been overtaxed, and fearing a return of the malaise that frequently plagued her, she had declined Mr. Darcy's offer to see the sights.

"But, Lizzy, *you* must go," Jane said. "I would feel guilty if you remained at the villa on my account."

"Miss Elizabeth, I can assure you that the servants are most attentive," Darcy said, "and your sister will be properly looked after." Lizzy nodded, indicating that she would go ahead with her plans to tour the city. "So where shall we begin?"

"If it is I who is allowed to choose," Elizabeth answered, "then may we begin at the Duomo?"

"Of course."

"Will Alexa be joining you?" Jane asked. On the journey to Florence, she had noticed Alexa's excessive attention to her father. The child went so far as to refuse Jane's offer to have Alexa ride with Cassie in the Bingley carriage. Fortunately, since their arrival at the villa, the child had busied herself with Cassie, but would she agree to being left behind for a whole day?

"The answer to your question, Mrs. Bingley, is yes *and* no. Alexa's former nursemaid has married and has a child. She lives within easy walking distance of the Duomo. I thought Alexa could come with us and visit with Clara, and Cassie is welcome as well."

Upon hearing Mr. Darcy's suggestion, Jane made a face, and Charles stared at his plate. Even he had noticed Alexa's preoccupation with her father and found it odd.

Glancing at his friends, Darcy added, "Alexa is very fond of Clara, and she has not seen her in quite a while," he said in defense of his decision, "nor has she seen the baby. Every child loves babies!"

"Can they not visit another day?" Jane asked.

Thus challenged, Darcy looked to Elizabeth. "Your sister and Bingley disagree with my decision, so please tell me, what do you think, Miss Elizabeth?"

Elizabeth hesitated, but then decided that she would answer the question honestly. "I believe that if you hope to succeed in establishing the different spheres inhabited by children and adults, you must stand firm. But if you do not wish to leave the child, I can see Florence on my own. While I was in Aix, I read an excellent guide on how best to view the sites of the city. All you have to do is stand in the Piazza della Signoria, and for a small fee, someone will guide you. Apparently, there are numerous art students from England living here in Florence who are eager for the employment."

Although Elizabeth had hoped for a repeat of the day Mr. Darcy and she had spent together in Livorno, knowing that she would never return to Florence, she refused to be denied the pleasure of seeing the sights because of the insecurities of a six-year-old child. Surely Mr. Darcy was in a position to provide an escort for her into the city.

"That is true about the guides," Darcy responded, "but if you chose to go that route, I would have failed in my duty as your host." Although said in a soft voice, his unhappiness with her plan was evident. "I have no wish to alarm you, Miss Elizabeth, but Florence is a city known for cutpurses and pickpockets. These thieves are always on the lookout for targets, most particularly innocents abroad, especially those of the female sex."

Now regretting her statement, Elizabeth looked down at her hands. On her very first day in Florence, she had managed to offend her host. Uncomfortable with the ensuing silence, Jane suggested that they all go into the city, but Darcy shook his head.

"If my statement sounded like a rebuke, I apologize. Please forgive a man who is struggling in the role of being the sole parent to a child who is quite capable of wrapping her dear Papa around her small finger," he said, looking at each of his guests in their turn. "So it is agreed. On the morrow, Miss Elizabeth and I will view the Duomo, and Alexa will remain with Mrs. Bingley."

Chapter 13

Elizabeth awoke to the smell of bread cooking in the villa's kitchen, reminding her of the delicious bread they had enjoyed the previous evening when a local dish, *ribollita,* a ham soup with beans, olive oil, and seasonal vegetables, had been served, and they were soon to learn that there were few dishes that did not have beans and olive oil as ingredients.

As Elizabeth lay in her canopied bed, she thought of what the day would bring and started to giggle at her good fortune. Not only was she in Florence, but she was the guest of Mr. Fitzwilliam Darcy. Although their time together would be limited to a few short weeks, she would relish it because once she returned to England, she would assume the mantle of the old-maid sister. Within her hearing, people would discuss her unenviable situation. They would repeat claims that she had once been reported to be a beauty but her good looks had proved insufficient to overcome her lack of a dowry.

While seeing to her morning toilette, Elizabeth noticed that there were several small watercolors propped up on easels placed around the bedchamber. Upon closer examination, she saw Amelie Darcy's signature in the corner and realized that this bedchamber had once belonged to Mr. Darcy's wife. With its unequaled view of the gardens and the Tuscan hills, it was easy to understand why Amelie Darcy had chosen this room, and Elizabeth was flattered to think that Mr. Darcy had wanted her to have the same view.

Now that she was aware of the room's former occupant, Elizabeth viewed the chamber with different eyes, and she looked for traces of the late Mrs. Darcy. In the bottom drawer of the dressing table was a bottle of Galimard perfume in an exquisite cut-crystal bottle. After removing its top, she inhaled its fragrance, but only a faint smell of roses lingered. Next to the perfume was a beautiful lace cap, one that Mrs. Darcy would have worn to indicate her status as a married woman, and several embroidered handkerchiefs. The remaining drawers were a disappointment as they contained only those items that would be used by a guest of the villa. If any clues were to be gathered about Amelie Darcy, she must look to her paintings.

Having tried her hand at painting watercolors, Elizabeth recognized Mrs. Darcy's talent in depicting landscapes as the lady had succeeded in capturing the light, most particularly the light created by the blue mist that was unique to the Florentine hills, a most difficult task for an amateur painter. There were also scenes of the Fountain of the Four Dolphins and views of Montagne Sainte Victorie from her time spent in Aix.

But as the mother of a young child, surely there were drawings of Alexa.

Elizabeth looked about for a sketchbook and found it in the bottom drawer of the wardrobe. As expected, there were numerous sketches of Alexa and several of Amelie's mother, father, and sister. Mr. and Mrs. Cantwell looked very much like Jack Sprat and his wife, and a lovely Eugenie favored her younger sister in all but the color of her hair. Although the portraits showed a degree of competence, they did not match the skill of Mrs. Darcy's landscapes. Thumbing through the pages while looking for a sketch of Mr. Darcy, she found only one: an incomplete charcoal, and she understood why it had been abandoned. His countenance was too severe, his jaw too square, his eyes too cold. After examining the sketch, she thought she must not read too much into one drawing. Perhaps Mrs. Darcy had realized that she was incapable of capturing the essence of her husband and had turned her attention to landscapes. While returning the sketchbook to the drawer, Elizabeth wondered how Mr. Darcy had fared with his daughter. She was soon to have her answer.

Upon entering the dining room, she noted Mr. Darcy's pinched look, evidence that things had not gone well with Alexa. She truly felt sorry for the man. With his wife gone, his daughter's care fell entirely to him. The only solution for his dilemma was not the hiring of a governess, but in finding a wife who would take over the responsibility of Alexa's care, and that would not happen until he returned to England. Once back in his home country, with his superior rank and considerable wealth, Mr. Darcy would have no difficulty in choosing a bride from a bounty of rich widows or newly-minted debutantes. But that solution was far in the future. In the meantime, it was Elizabeth's intention to enjoy Florence as his guest.

* * *

The day began in the Piazza della Signoria at the Loggia dei Lanzi, an open-air gallery, whose curved arches provided shelter for several epic sculptures, including *Perseus and the Head of Medusa*, as well as the *Rape of the Sabine Women*, both statues providing compelling reminders of the power of the Medicis and the consequences for defiance. After enjoying the cool mist of the Neptune fountain, they turned their attention to the sculpture of *David* that dominated the piazza.

"Look at the tension in his neck, the fixed gaze, and furrowed brow," Elizabeth said, pointing to the colossus with his marble curls framing his face. "Michelangelo has captured David just moments before he releases his missile and slays the giant. What an accomplishment!" she said, standing in awe of the man who had freed the image from its stone prison.

Although she would have liked to have spent more time with the shepherd boy and his friends under the loggia, the Duomo beckoned.

The basilica, built to honor Santa Maria del Fiore, Our Lady of the Flowers, was enormous. As much as there was to admire on its intricate western façade, because the hottest part of the day was already upon them, they entered through the central portal into its cool interior. Once inside the Duomo, it was almost too much to take in. Between the intricate mosaic of the tile flooring and its soaring dome, Elizabeth felt miniscule. But wasn't that the architect's intention? The humble, insignificant pilgrim praying at the altar of the almighty God.

"You can go up to the dome, you know," Darcy said. "From there, you will have the best view of Vasari's frescoes through the portals. I shall warn you. Many people experience vertigo."

"Surely, it is worth the risk!"

Darcy smiled at her enthusiasm. "After walking through a stone labyrinth, you will exit the church's interior, and from there, you will see the most glorious scene in the whole world. But you must earn it! It is a climb of nearly five hundred steps."

"Do you not remember, Mr. Darcy? I am an excellent walker."

"I remember commenting upon your enthusiasm for the exercise when you visited Netherfield to nurse your sister."

"That was a long time ago."

"Yes, it does seem like a lifetime ago, but there is very little from that time I have forgotten." And then he chuckled. "I particularly remember one conversation where you asked who was the first person to discover the efficacy of poetry in driving love away. At the time, I believed poetry to be the food of love, but you were of a different mind. You declared that of a stout and healthy love it was, but if it be only a thin sort of inclination, that one good sonnet would starve it entirely away."

Elizabeth remembered the remark and the day it was said. Her mother, accompanied by her younger sisters, had come to Netherfield Park, ostensibly to visit the ailing Jane, but Mrs. Bennet's real reason soon became evident. It was her intention to have her eldest remain at Netherfield, no matter how long it took, until she had succeeded in securing Mr. Bingley's affections. All attempts by Elizabeth to moderate or deflect her mother's comments had failed, resulting in considerable embarrassment on her part and a look of disgust from Mr. Darcy.

"May I offer a belated apology for my comment? I was trying to be clever, but, instead, I ended up spouting nonsense."

"You *were* clever and, as it turns out, correct. Poetry is the food of love only to those who wished to be nourished."

* * *

After viewing Vasari's frescoes, breathless, exhausted, and sweaty, Elizabeth emerged into the Florentine sunlight and removed her bonnet. She did not want anything to obscure her view of the baptistery, the campanile, the Piazza della Signoria, Ponte Vechhio, the River Arno, all there, in front of her, for her pleasure.

"It will be difficult for you to leave here," Elizabeth said, admiring the greatness of the city. "I have only been here two days, and I think I should never want to leave."

"I do not intend to undertake my journey home until mid September. By that time, I will be in need of a respite from the heat and humidity which will make it much easier to leave Florence, especially when my route takes me by way of Lake Lausanne to visit with my cousin, Colonel Fitzwilliam."

"How is your cousin?" Elizabeth asked of a man whose company she had enjoyed at Rosings Park.

"Very well indeed. He has had the good fortune to fall in love with a wealthy woman! They spend their summers on Lake Lausanne and their winters in a villa overlooking the Bay of Naples."

Elizabeth was pleased to hear of the colonel's good fortune. Unlike Mr. Darcy, Colonel Fitzwilliam was not of a taciturn nature, and they had enjoyed several lively discussions at Rosings Park. She repeated a conversation she had had with the colonel in which he had declared that younger sons of earls could not marry without some attention to money.

"I understood his predicament but mentioned that younger sons very often found themselves in the company of women of fortune. He understood my remarks were not meant to criticize, but merely to highlight the difficulties of finding suitable marriage partners for those with little money."

"But money is but one consideration in choosing a partner."

"Yes, I understand that men from your social circle must find a bride who is their equal in rank."

"It is my opinion that shared interests and a meeting of the minds are infinitely more important than rank or a lady's dowry in determining conjugal felicity and domestic comfort."

"But we were speaking not of ladies, but of your cousin. As the younger son of an earl with certain habits of expense, Colonel Fitzwilliam was not in a position to ignore monetary considerations. Fortunately, the woman he married was in possession of a fortune, and I am very happy for the colonel as I liked him very much."

"And he liked you very much as well, and for that reason, I insisted we leave Rosings Park together."

Although confused by Mr. Darcy's response, his words brought up another memory: a time when the two gentlemen had come to the parsonage to take their leave of Mr. and Mrs. Collins before departing Rosings Park. Because she had yet to recover from the dreadful scene that had played out in the Collins's parlor, she had felt a sense of relief that she had not been at the parsonage at the time of their call. Although she regretted not having an opportunity to speak to the colonel, as for Mr. Darcy, at that time, her preference would have been to have seen him exiled to the far ends of the earth.

"Is Mrs. Fitzwilliam English?" Elizabeth asked, her thoughts returning to the present.

"No. Richard met her when he was briefly posted to Nova Scotia with his regiment. Apparently, there was some interest, because after her husband died, she wrote to the colonel, and he saw the benefits of the union. Fortunately, they are of such similar temperaments that they get along famously. It is a pleasure to be in their company to say nothing of having access to their excellent house on the lake and their villa in Naples."

"I am sure there is a great deal to see in Naples, but I can hardly imagine doing justice to what is available here in Florence."

"I agree it is a problem. Although I have seen much, there is still much that lays hidden. But I hope it will not be my last visit to Florence. When I again marry, I would want to share this view with my wife."

"Mr. Darcy, I hope that will happen very soon." Elizabeth could feel tears forming. "I do not think people are meant to go through life alone. You have loved once. Why should you not love again?"

"Yes, I have loved once." With that, Mr. Darcy looked away and pretended to admire the view, but Elizabeth could see that his thoughts were elsewhere and believed he was remembering another time when he had climbed these steps with his wife.

"What did Mrs. Darcy think of this view?" Elizabeth asked.

"Amelie never saw it."

Elizabeth imagined the reason was her poor health, but because Mr. Darcy added nothing to his comment, she asked no questions.

"It has been a full day, shall we?" he asked, gesturing towards the entrance to the Duomo.

Chapter 14

During the carriage ride to Le Torri Dorate, Elizabeth declined Mr. Darcy's offer of a return visit to the city the next day.

"Are you fatigued? Did I press you too hard?" Darcy asked, and then winced at his phrasing.

"Oh no! Not at all," Elizabeth answered, unaware of his embarrassment. She explained that she thought it best to spend the day with Cassie. Between the journey from Livorno and a day spent visiting the Duomo, Cassie had not been doing her lessons. But there was another reason: Alexa. The child's education was random—a lesson here, a lesson there, but little in the way of an established routine.

While dining at a roadside inn between Livorno and Florence, Elizabeth had suggested to Mr. Darcy that she be allowed to set up a classroom at the villa as she had done at her sister's home in Derby. Fully aware that his daughter needed a routine, he had readily agreed, and Elizabeth reminded Mr. Darcy of his agreement.

"You prefer the role of governess to that of tourist?" a surprised Darcy asked.

"Of course not! But I have agreed to see to Cassie's lessons and now Alexa's."

"As eager as I am for Alexa to learn to read and write and to do sums, it is equally important to feed the soul and nourish the spirit, and there is no better place to do that than in Florence."

Before proceeding, Darcy hesitated as if collecting his thoughts, and Elizabeth could see that something was truly troubling him.

"At times, I have stood in the Uffizi Gallery admiring a great painting, and I have heard others discuss brushstrokes and technique, and they *are* important. But if all that you see are the mechanics of the painting, then you have missed the point.

"I shall admit that there have been times in my life when I concentrated on the brushstrokes. As the grandson of an earl, I thought I must do everything that was expected of the future Master of Pemberley. I must receive a gentleman's education, and so I had tutors and language and dancing masters and studied at Cambridge. I learned how to ride and shoot and excel at games. But by concentrating on the brushstrokes, another part of my education was neglected. Although I was given good principles, I was left to follow them in pride and conceit.

"It took... It took another to show me that it is not only the brushstrokes that matter, but the finished painting, that is, the grown man. Am I deserving of the respect of my tenants, my neighbors, my friends? Am I a man who is worthy of the love of my child? The love of a good woman? If I am not, then all the many hours spent in the classroom or perfecting these skills were wasted."

"Mr. Darcy, you are too hard on yourself," Elizabeth said, leaning forward on her seat, their knees almost touching. "If you believe that you erred as a young man, I am quite confident in saying that you have reformed. The man, the finished painting, is a gentleman worthy of admiration. One only has to see you with your daughter to know the depth of your ability to love and be loved."

"Yes, Miss Elizabeth, Alexa loves me, but is that all that is left to me? The love of my child? I hope not."

Chapter 15

For someone who had expressed little interest in going
into Florence, Jane was demanding a detailed account of
Elizabeth's day. Although she would have preferred to
have had time to herself to savor her time with Mr.
Darcy, Jane would not be denied, and her questions
included the minutiae of a delicious meal they had
enjoyed at a *trattoria* that was little bigger than the
kitchen at Longbourn. After two glasses of Chianti, a
looser Mr. Darcy had shared stories of his years on the
Continent, including swimming, in April, in an Alpine
lake.

"I did it on a dare," Darcy explained. "I was visiting
with Colonel Fitzwilliam, and he provoked me into
doing it. It is, to date, the stupidest thing I have ever
done as the lake was filled with melting snow. I was
only in the water five minutes, but it took five hours to
scrape the frost off of me!"

After their meal, they had returned to the Duomo so
that they might view its interior in the late afternoon
light, and the allotted time had permitted only a few

brief minutes viewing the bronze doors of the baptistery.

"During the carriage ride to Le Torri Dorate, I spoke with Mr. Darcy about setting up a classroom for the children in the root cellar." Elizabeth shared with her sister that gentleman's opinion on the matter. "He views the whole of Florence as a classroom."

Jane wore a puzzled look.

"Perhaps Mr. Darcy's view on his daughter's education can best be explained by a memory he shared with me. As a lad touring the Continent with his father, Mr. Darcy stood under the dome of the Pantheon in Rome. Because of his youth, he was incapable of understanding its engineering and mathematical complexities. Nonetheless, a seed had been planted and proved to be an inspiration for his own studies of architecture at Cambridge and for some architectural changes he made at Pemberley. Although he wishes for his daughter to master the basics, he also wants us to plant seeds—to feed the spirit as well as the mind."

Jane continued to be perplexed. After much thought, she declared that she preferred a different analogy. "Rather than planting seeds, would it not be better for us to provide a strong foundation on which to build? Once we have done that, then Cassie and Alexa's curiosity may lead them in other directions. But in the end, does it make any difference?" Jane asked, shaking her head. "We are not speaking of a young man of fortune and rank, whose opportunities are boundless and who might study whatever he wants at Oxford or Cambridge, but two little girls. Their success in society will be measured by their accomplishments, their ability to speak Italian or French, to play an instrument, or to demonstrate a talent in singing, all with an eye to making a good match."

Elizabeth could not argue with Jane's reasoning. Due to her own failure to marry well, her world had now shrunk to a root cellar in Florence that was to be remade into a classroom.

With the discussion regarding the children now concluded, Jane wanted to know if Elizabeth felt awkward being in Mr. Darcy's company without a chaperone and if their situation had attracted any attention.

"The only reaction from the native population was one of annoyance. Enthralled by the fantastic art in the piazza, tourists tend to come to a complete stop in front of a piece of art oblivious to what is going on around them. As a result, the Florentines must move their carts around these bothersome visitors. There is no mistaking their unhappiness with *L'Inglese* as their displeasure is acted out in loud protests and dramatic gestures. It may be one of the few times when my inability to speak Italian might be viewed as an asset."

"What monuments did you visit?" Jane asked, laughing at her sister's comment.

After summarizing their time spent at the Duomo, she mentioned the sculptures under the Loggia dei Lanzi.

"Honestly, Jane, Medusa's head was so realistic, I found myself looking at the pavement for traces of blood. And there was also a complex composition of two men and a woman called the *Rape of the Sabine Women*."

"Rape? What a subject for a sculpture!" Jane said in disapproval.

"In this case, 'rape' means 'abduction.' In Rome's past, the way the men chose a wife was to raid a neighboring tribe and to take their women. In this particular pose, a man is lifting his victim high above him, and she is crying out, and with good reason. I would cry out if I was being carried away by a brute who had stripped me of my clothes!"

"Stripped me of my clothes? Whatever do you mean?"

"The Sabine is naked as are most of the subjects of these statutes." Jane was clearly surprised by this revelation. "Surely you knew Michelangelo's *David* was a nude."

"How would I know that?"

"Everyone knows that! *David* is one of the most famous sculptures in the world. It is in an art book in the library at Netherfield Park."

"I shall have to take your word for it as the only books I read from Netherfield's library were Maria Edgeworth's novels. Now tell me, how nude is *David*?" Jane asked. When Elizabeth described the sculpture, she broke out into a fit of giggling. "How could you stare at the naked body of a man with Mr. Darcy standing next to you? Did you not look away?"

"Look away from a seventeen-foot statue? I would like to see you try. Just picture three Charleses, without so much a thread on, standing one on top of the other. Try ignoring that!"

"Was everything in proportion?" Jane asked, starting to giggle.

"No, not everything. There was something that was most definitely larger than average."

At this point, the sisters were nearly hysterical. "How would you know what is average?"

"Because I have seen hundreds of them." Jane's eyes were now open wide. "Of course, I am referring to *David's* hands."

After the two had dried their tears of laughter, Elizabeth spoke of how pleasant the day had been. Mr. Darcy had been the perfect host, providing just enough history to make sense of all she was seeing without robbing the art of its intrinsic beauty.

"I think tomorrow whilst I see to the girls' lessons, you and Charles should go into town with Mr. Darcy and see the sights. At the very least, you should go to the Piazza della Signoria."

Jane's enthusiasm did not equal her sister's. "Frankly, I am enjoying the villa's superb gardens, and despite the warm weather, I feel invigorated. This afternoon, I actually chased after the girls—not for long, mind you—but I was pleased that I could do it at all.

Besides, Charles cannot go into Florence tomorrow as Mr. Darcy has made arrangements for him to go shooting—at what, I do not know."

"I am pleased to hear it. Charles was so looking forward to it."

"Now that Mr. Darcy will not be going into Florence with you, I imagine he will join Charles. This may be a lost opportunity on your part, Lizzy."

"Jane, please do not imagine a romance between Mr. Darcy and me." To make her point, Elizabeth repeated the words Mr. Darcy had spoken at the top of the Duomo—that it was his intention to take a wife.

"Does he have anyone in mind?"

"Not that he would mention to me."

"Then all is well."

"Jane, please do not do this! Mr. Darcy does not love me. For you to plot and plan a romance that cannot be would be hurtful. Do you understand?"

Jane nodded. Although the last thing she wanted to do was to cause her sister pain, there was no forgetting the past. There had been a time when Mr. Darcy had asked Elizabeth to be his wife. Why should he not ask again?

Chapter 16

With the realization that she had only a few weeks to make a difference in Alexa's life, Elizabeth quickly set about her task. With an eye toward turning a possible challenger into an ally, she enlisted Miss Darcy's help in setting up the classroom. The room chosen had once served as a place to store fruits, vegetables, and herbs for the kitchen until a cellar was dug for that purpose nearer to the house. Because of its location on the north side of the property, it escaped the worst of the heat.

Alexa was not just helpful, but enthusiastic. After a day spent moving tables and chairs and gathering supplies necessary for a classroom, Elizabeth thanked Miss Darcy for her assistance. With her big blues orbs looking directly into Elizabeth's dark eyes, Alexa explained that because Miss Elizabeth was her guest, she must be a considerate hostess and do all that was asked of her. After all, she explained, she wished for Miss Elizabeth to have good memories of her time in Florence. The implication was clear: I shall be here with Papa long after you have returned to England.

Unsettled by a six-year-old hatching such a scheme, Elizabeth sought Jane's advice, but rather than being concerned by Alexa's plotting, Jane thought it was all to her sister's benefit.

"I assume Alexa is ignorant of her father's plans to return to England at the end of the summer?"

Elizabeth nodded. "In the carriage yesterday, Mr. Darcy told me that he will 'break the news' to his daughter when he returns from Pistoia in August. And please do not mention the Palio in front of Alexa as he has yet to tell her that he will be leaving for a few weeks. He sees no benefit in having her dwell on his departure for such a long time. I only hope he goes. If he thinks too much on what his absence will mean to Alexa, he might very well reconsider it as his original plans were to have Charles go to Pistoia with his neighbor, Count Bardi, and for him to remain here at the villa."

"Do not worry about his going to Pistoia. Charles will shame him into it," Jane said as if such pressure assured Mr. Darcy's attendance. "As far as Alexa is concerned, because she thinks you are a temporary nuisance, she will behave herself, and you will be able to run your classroom without difficulty."

Elizabeth could only hope that Jane was right. "If I am successful in establishing a schedule for Alexa, when she returns to England, her governess will have a pattern to follow." After thinking of Mr. Darcy's comment about her preference for being a governess over a tourist, she added, "However, it is my intention to have the children in the classroom only three days a week. In that way, I shall be able to go into Florence to visit the sights."

* * *

Soon after their arrival at Le Torri Dorate, the visitors had adapted to the realities of a warm climate. Every planned activity revolved around the heat and humidity of a Florentine summer. As soon as the guests had finished their breakfast, they were hard at whatever had been planned for that day. If the men were to ride, they would be in the carriage that would take them to the stables of their neighbor, Count Roberto Bardi. If they were to go into Florence, the driver would have been alerted the previous night so that the conveyance would be ready and waiting. On days when there were lessons, Elizabeth and the children would take their morning exercise in the gardens before going to the classroom to avoid the hottest part of the day. Late afternoons were dedicated to enjoying the sacrosanct siesta.

In early afternoon, a light meal would be taken and a more substantial repast enjoyed once the sun dipped below the horizon, a time when shuttered windows were thrown open to let in the cool breezes of their hilltop villa. After an evening spent playing charades or other games for the benefit of the children, Elizabeth would oversee their bedtime ritual that always ended with a story. Sometimes Elizabeth would read from a book, but at other times, Alexa and Cassie were allowed to make up their own tales, which usually involved a handsome prince rescuing a beautiful princess imprisoned in a golden tower.

Evenings were spent on the terrace or in the drawing room where Jane performed on the villa's excellent pianoforte with Elizabeth often accompanying her. Frequently, in lieu of cards, Mr. Darcy invited Elizabeth to play backgammon. At present, Elizabeth led nine games to eight, but she had been in Mr. Darcy's company long enough to know how very competitive he was and that he would continue to challenge her until he took the lead.

After anticipating a difficult start in her role as Alexa's tutor, Elizabeth was surprised to find that the child was cooperative and eager to learn. Initially viewing Elizabeth as a threat, Alexa's suspicions had been allayed when Elizabeth and Mr. Darcy went into Florence to see the sights and returned with no harm done.

On their first outing to the Duomo, as soon as her father had stepped foot out of the carriage, the child had hugged the man as if he had just returned from a six-month sea voyage. As had been the case in Livorno, Elizabeth expected Alexa to stay glued to her father's side for the remainder of the day, but the child had surprised both of them by returning to the company of Cassandra Bingley so that the pair could continue their chase of the numerous cats that were to be found in every dark corner on the property. This scene was repeated after every excursion into the city.

With the children content to remain at the villa in the care of Flora, the daughter of Signor and Signora Moncini, the caretaker and cook, the four adults were free to go into Florence. When the men were otherwise engaged, Mr. Darcy made arrangements for Signor Ciampi, the notario used by Mr. Darcy in connection with the lease of the villa, to act as their escort, the notario's English-born wife, Signora Ciampi, serving as their guide at the Uffizi.

Without Charles by her side, Jane had agreed to go to the gallery only after being assured that she would not have to view the naked colossus of *David* or the other nudes featured in the piazza. "Keep your eyes down," was Elizabeth's best advice as *all* of the statues were in some state of undress.

When Elizabeth mentioned Jane's concerns to Signora Ciampi, the woman suggested that if Mrs. Bingley's modesty prevented her from viewing a naked boy carved in cold white marble, it would be best to avoid Titian's vibrant *Venus of Urbino* that left nothing to the imagination.

"The painting is known as a reclining nude—nude, as in, not a stitch of clothing," Signora Ciampi explained. "The model used by Titian was a celebrated Venetian courtesan and companion of the artist. There is speculation that the painting once decorated the bedchamber of the Duchess of Urbino to serve as a tutorial for the young bride of the duke."

A tutorial! Knowing nothing of what went on behind the closed doors of a married couple, Elizabeth

111

would have to find a way to view the painting without Jane knowing of it.

"I hope your sister's modesty will not prevent her from enjoying Boticelli's *Birth of Venus*. It is not nearly as suggestive as the Titian, and it is one of the glories of the Uffizi. And, of course, no one can leave Florence without viewing the Tribuna, the room where the statute of the *Venus d' Medici* is displayed. If we are to see it, we should hurry as the art students will be setting up their easels making it very difficult to move about. There are that many of them."

The signora was correct. The Tribuna was already crowded with amateurs painting copies of the great art displayed on its walls with varying degrees of success. The most talented would succeed in selling copies to the hordes of English and German tourists who frequented the gallery, while most would paint over the canvas and begin again.

In order to distract Jane from Titian's *Venus*, which was prominently displayed on an easel near the entrance to the room, Signora Ciampi pointed to a painting high on the wall of the octagonal room, but after viewing the painting, Jane's eyes settled on a statue of a nude dancing faun, and she immediately retreated.

"Jane, do not be silly," Elizabeth said after joining her sister in the long gallery. "You are a married woman. The anatomy of a male cannot possibly be shocking to you."

"When it belongs to someone other than my husband, I can assure you that I am quite capable of being shocked."

"Then look at the faun's head."

"It is not his head that is at eye level," Jane said in a whisper.

"Then look at the *Venus d' Medici*," Elizabeth said, taking Jane by the hand and returning to the room where the statue was housed. "Is she not beautiful?" Elizabeth thought the sculpture of the goddess of love emerging from the waters was one of the most beautiful things she had ever seen. Even an unsettled Jane agreed that the statue was lovely, so much so, that as Elizabeth wandered about the room admiring the Tribuna's bounty, Jane stayed riveted to a spot in front of the *Venus*.

With Jane thus occupied, Elizabeth made her way to the front of the room where Titian's *Venus* was being admired by a largely male audience who were explicit in their descriptions of her attributes. After looking at the reclining nude, Elizabeth turned scarlet, thus producing a chuckle from Signora Ciampi.

"Well, what do you have to say about this magnificent painting, Miss Bennet?"

"Um. I think it is..." Elizabeth stopped. She really did not know what to think about a woman as naked as Eve leaving the garden, but who, unlike Eve, was unashamed of her nakedness. In fact, the whole purpose of the painting was to advertise her assets. "All I can say is that I hope the room was warm!"

"Oh, I shall have to tell my husband that one," Signora Ciampi said, laughing out loud.

"Quickly," Elizabeth said, leading the signora away from the painting. "Jane is coming, and I think she would die of embarrassment if she saw the *Venus* whilst in mixed company."

After an afternoon spent admiring the works of Michelangelo, Raphael, Fra Filippo Lippi, and the other Old Masters, Elizabeth, Jane, and their guide rejoined Signor Ciampi who had spent his time outside one of the many trattorias near the gallery along with other neglected husbands. Although sitting erect, the man was most definitely asleep as his head was bobbing, and who could blame him? With an open wine bottle and the remnants of a meal providing evidence of a full stomach, he had drifted off, lulled to sleep by the warm breezes of the piazza.

The sound of the ladies joining the signor caused the man to catapult out of his seat, and he quickly ordered a board of bread and cheese and three glasses so that he might share his Chianti. After exchanging a few pleasantries, the notario excused himself, and his wife explained that he was embarrassed by his poor English. Despite having lived in England for a dozen years, he had failed to learn the language.

"When transacting business with the English who come to Florence and lease villas, I serve as my husband's translator," Signora Ciampi explained, "but with Mr. Darcy, because his Italian is excellent, it is never a problem."

"Miss Darcy's Italian is also excellent," Jane added. "We quite rely on her when speaking with Signora Moncini, Mr. Darcy's cook."

"The late Mrs. Darcy relied on the little girl as well, as she spoke only enough Italian to discuss the menus with Signora Moncini," the notario's wife added, "her primary language being French."

"French!" Jane said. "Mrs. Darcy was English."

Although Jane understood that people of the upper class often spoke French in polite society, their native tongue was English.

"She was English only by accident of birth," Signora Ciampi said. Although the signora laughed, there was nothing friendly about it.

Elizabeth shared with Jane a conversation she had had with Mr. Darcy in which he explained that Mr. Cantwell, Amelie Darcy's father, was a representative of His Majesty's government in Bordeaux and had married the daughter of a vicomte. During the uprisings of the Revolution, they had been forced to flee to England with Mrs. Darcy's older sister.

"Although born in England, Mrs. Darcy declared that French blood ran in her veins," the signora said, taking back the story. "Because Mrs. Darcy's mother was French and her father fluent in the language, it was the family's practice to speak French in their home.

Mrs. Darcy said that by speaking French it was the best way for Alexa to learn the language. So much easier than hiring a French tutor, she said, and having a stranger in the villa. Mr. Darcy was less keen on the idea as his daughter was beginning to think of herself as French, not English."

"But Florence is not France," Jane said confused.

"As often as Mrs. Darcy's mother and sister visited Le Torri Dorate, it might as well have been France. I believe the presence of the in-laws was the main reason why Mr. Darcy wanted to go back to England. Despite his wishes, if Mrs. Darcy had lived, I do not think it would have happened," Signora Ciampi said, shaking her head. "It was never the lady's intention to live in England. As far as she was concerned, Derbyshire was at the end of the world."

"I am sure Mrs. Darcy's objection to going back to England had more to do with her poor health than Derbyshire being 'at the end of the world,'" Jane said, and Elizabeth could hear annoyance inching into her sister's voice.

"I am sure you are right, dear," the lady said, patting Jane's hand, but it was said in such a way as to leave the impression that she, Signora Ciampi, was right, and Jane wrong.

During the exchange, Elizabeth had been watching their guide, and there was no mistaking that the woman was no fan of Amelie Darcy. Believing it was wrong to talk about Mrs. Darcy under any circumstance, but most especially with a woman whom they had only met earlier that day, Elizabeth placed her hand on her sister's sleeve to let her know that the discussion should come to an end.

"Let us speak of other things," Elizabeth suggested. "Whilst in the Uffizi, I overheard a conversation in which the parties indicated that the British Consul is to return to Florence and host a reception in mid August at the Consulate."

"I have not heard anything," Signora Ciampi snapped, "and I think it unlikely as Sir Martin dislikes the heat and spends most of the summer on Lake Garda enjoying the company of his hostess, Signora Fontini, amongst others."

From her tone, the signora left no doubt that she considered Signora Fontini to be more than just a hostess, and in case her point had missed its mark, she added that Sir Martin's wife remained in England. But there was more tittle-tattle to share. Although Elizabeth and Jane had no knowledge of the English community living in Florence, Signora Ciampi introduced the major players who would be in attendance at any Consul reception, all of whom, according to the signora, had a hint of scandal attached to their names. It would seem that Florence's English community was made up entirely of unfaithful husbands and flirting wives. Obviously, the woman relished repeating tales of scandal, reminding Elizabeth of her Aunt Phillips and her cronies, Meryton's entrenched gossips. As soon as

Signora Ciampi's husband re-appeared, Elizabeth insisted they return to the villa.

During the carriage ride home, Elizabeth hoped to avoid any discussion of Mrs. Darcy, but Jane was disturbed by some of Signora Ciampi's comments, most particularly her harrumph when Jane mentioned Amelie Darcy's poor health.

"Similar to my experience with Cassie, Mrs. Darcy endured a difficult delivery," her defender asserted. "She indicated that the experience had left her suffering from a loss of appetite and constant fatigue—a sense of *ennui*, as she called it. You have met her, Elizabeth. She *was* very thin and ate like a bird."

"I think there is little doubt Mrs. Darcy suffered from poor health because I can hardly believe Mr. Darcy would have traveled hither and yon in search of a cure if he did not believe his wife's complaints were genuine." Jane nodded in agreement. "So are we agreed that we shall have no more discussion about Mrs. Darcy? I am truly uncomfortable in discussing the late wife of our host."

"But you do understand that Signora Ciampi was implying that…"

While Jane talked, Elizabeth looked out the carriage window trying to catch glimpses of the City of Flowers, her mind intent on not considering the possibility that Mr. Darcy had been married to a woman who had used false claims of ill health so that she might live anywhere but in England.

Chapter 17

For the benefit of the gentlemen, at supper, Jane shared the news that a reception was to be held at the British Consulate and boldly asked Mr. Darcy if he had received an invitation, giving the impression that she wished for the Bingley name to appear on the guest list as well.

Elizabeth could hardly believe that Jane would ask so personal a question of someone as private as Mr. Darcy, but upon reflection, she understood the change. Once Jane had learned of his kindness to Lydia during the elopement fiasco with George Wickham, her opinion of Mr. Darcy had been transformed. In one minute, he had gone from her husband's overbearing friend to benevolent knight.

A second possible reason for the change was his gracious hospitality. If Elizabeth, Jane, or Charles expressed a desire to see or do anything, Mr. Darcy ensured that it was done. Nothing, however small, was beneath his notice. Considering his many kindnesses and general civility, Elizabeth was surprised when Mr.

Darcy made reference to their difficult past during their ride into Florence:

"I was hoping to show you, by every civility in my power, that I am not so mean as to resent the past."

"Then you have succeeded," Elizabeth had answered. Although Mr. Darcy's speech at Hunsford was worthy of reproach, an examination of her own behavior had found much to criticize as well. "The conduct of neither of us, if strictly examined, is irreproachable. With the passage of so much time, perhaps it is best to leave the past in the past."

Elizabeth's thoughts were interrupted by Mr. Darcy's response to Jane's tacit request for an invitation to attend the Consul reception. "You will be happy to hear that this afternoon an invitation was delivered from the Office of the British Consul and addressed to 'Mr. Darcy and Guests.'"

"Oh, how wonderful! I had not thought to be included," Jane said, truly pleased.

Elizabeth was sure that her sister was already imagining herself in one of the new gowns and hats she had commissioned in Paris.

"As pleased as you are by the invitation, Mrs. Bingley, you do not know the best part. Sir Martin's receptions feature only the best Florentine wines and delicacies, and after dining on such fare, a local specialty, Buontalenti cream, is served. It is an iced cream that was created by Bernardo Buontalenti, an architect in the service of the Grand Duke of Tuscany, and the designer of Boboli Gardens. In my experience, there is nothing that can compare with this particular confection. They say the secret is the addition of sweet wine."

Mr. Darcy could not have addressed a more receptive audience. From childhood, Jane was teased that her natural sweetness came from her having a sweet tooth, and it appeared that Cassie had inherited the trait. It was a joy to see mother and daughter sharing an iced treat in one of Florence's many *gelato* shops.

"What is the date on the invitation?" Jane asked. Noting the date, she asked if Charles and he would have returned from Pistoia.

"Barring some epic weather event, I can assure you that we will be at the reception. One reason why I am so confident is that Bingley and I, by arrangement with Sir Martin, will be in Pistoia as the guest of the mayor. Sir Martin is also a Palio enthusiast and will be in attendance. If he lingers too long, we shall send him on his way so that he might see to the preparations for the reception."

"Oh, that *is* reassuring, Mr. Darcy," Jane said, laughing.

"The Pistoia Palio is one of many. On June 23, the eve of the feast of St. John, the Palio dei Cocchi is celebrated here in Florence in the Piazza Santa Maria Novella."

"Are women permitted to attend these events?" Elizabeth asked.

"Women are not excluded, but unless a view of the race can be arranged from one of the townhouses fronting the piazza, I would not recommend it for a woman of gentle birth."

"Oh, I have no wish to go!" Jane said, thinking of a square filled with the unwashed.

"I hope you are not entertaining any thoughts of attending," Mr. Darcy said to Elizabeth. "With Bingley and I both being absent, it would be necessary to arrange for an escort as it is not uncommon for young blades to take liberties with the ladies. Because their identities are hidden by the large crowds, their getaway is assured."

Elizabeth's mind turned to the crowded Piazza della Signoria where a young man had dared to slip his hands around her waist before feeling the weight of Signora Ciampi's umbrella.

"Oh, no... I only meant to inquire...," Elizabeth stuttered. "No, I do not wish to attend. May we change the subject?"

The conversation then turned to the ladies' day in Florence. With most of their time having been spent viewing nudes of both sexes, neither Elizabeth nor Jane knew what to say. How did one discuss the *Venus d' Medici* or the *Marble Faun* in the company of gentlemen?

From Mr. Darcy's smile, it was obvious he had guessed the reason for their reticence. "Did you have an opportunity to visit the Tribuna?" Both ladies nodded.

"Then, of course, you saw the magnificent *Venus d' Medici*. It was inspired by the statue of *Aphrodite* by Praxiteles. Because of its beauty and subject, admirers voyaged to the Greek isle of Knidos to view her. Legend has it that Nicomedes of Bithynia offered to pay off all the debts of the city of Knidos in exchange for the statue, but the Knidians rejected his offer, refusing to let go of their beautiful *Aphrodite*."

"Good grief!" Bingley said. "Pay off a city's debts just so you could own a particular statute! If I were the ruler of Knidos, I would have accepted the offer and got another statue."

"If you had been with us today, Charles, you would be of a different mind!" Jane said revealing her own attachment to the *Venus*.

"I see that the *Venus* has claimed another admirer," Darcy said, addressing Mrs. Bingley. "Another reason why the Knidians were so keen to keep the statute is that it was the first female nude in the ancient world."

"Well, in that case, I might have held on to it!" Charles said, laughing.

Although Jane laughed at her husband's comment, Elizabeth's face flamed, and an amused Darcy apologized if he had embarrassed her.

"Not at all, Mr. Darcy," Elizabeth said, a statement clearly at odds with her flushed face. "We were speaking of art which requires a different sensibility. I, too, was enchanted by the *Venus*."

"Whilst in the Tribuna," Jane continued, "I overheard several discussions about her modest gestures, but the look on her face is not just a result of her modesty. She is also worried."

"About what?" Darcy asked, intrigued.

"She had just emerged from the waves into a world unknown to her. As she cautiously looks about, she asks, 'Who is nearby?' 'Who can see me?' 'Are there those who will do me harm?' All these things appear in her look."

"Although I have seen the *Venus* a dozen times, I must confess I never thought of her in that way, Mrs. Bingley."

"How do you see her, sir?"

"I see her as a woman who knew how to use her beauty to get what she wanted. Although she enjoyed the act of falling in love, the ability to maintain the relationship eluded her, and she looked for amusement elsewhere."

"Possibly so," Jane added. "But that is not the moment captured by the artist."

Turning to Elizabeth, he asked her opinion of the *Venus*.

"I must confess that I spent my time admiring the artist's skill. I looked for no deeper meaning."

"Sometimes that is best."

Chapter 18

With each day a wonder of discovery, Elizabeth felt that there was no place on earth she would rather be than in Florence. On days when Cassie and Alexa had lessons, all would eat breakfast *al fresco* on the terrace before going into the gardens for a morning spent playing games, usually chase or blind man's bluff. Elizabeth took pleasure in watching Charles and Mr. Darcy pretend not to know where their daughters were hiding or to sneak up behind them and listen to the girls squeal in delight.

Once in the classroom, lessons began in earnest, and Cassie and Alexa's parents often visited to listen to their children recite a poem or read a passage from a primer. Mr. Darcy was particularly keen to have Alexa study the history and geography of England and would quiz her on what she had learned.

"Alexa, what is the largest city in England?"

"London, Papa."

"What is the greatest river in England?"

"The Thames. And the largest city in Derbyshire is Derby, and the longest river is the Derwent. A tribulary…"

"Tributary," her father corrected her.

"A tributary of the Derwent runs through Pemberley."

"Please show me all of these places on the map."

In the few weeks that Elizabeth had served as Alexa's tutor, she had come to the conclusion that if the child heard it, saw it, or read it, she retained it. In keeping with Mr. Darcy's wishes, Alexa was allowed to speak on topics of interest to her, but despite her father's wishes to "engage the spirit" and have the world become her classroom, the subjects chosen were more of prose than poetry. Unlike Mr. Darcy, who, at a young age, had admired the architecture of ancient Rome, Alexa's interests were less grandiose, a good deal of them having to do with the cats that roamed the property or the fishermen who cast their nets into the Arno, and she was rather fond of turning over rocks in the hopes of finding some creature hidden beneath.

While Elizabeth oversaw the children's studies, Jane had offered to supervise the girls' lessons on the pianoforte as well as their singing lessons. On a day when no lessons were planned, Elizabeth suggested that they take the children into Florence. Much to Cassie and Alexa's relief, their destination was to be the fruit and vegetable markets of San Lorenzo and not the basilica that housed the tombs of the Medicis and that gave the square its name.

Every stall of the mercato was filled to overflowing with delights for every taste. While Alexa and Cassie eyed table grapes, Elizabeth and Jane filled their baskets with arugula, spinach, broccoli, and zucchini for the Le Torri Dorate cook. They also visited the leather and gold markets, and both ladies were fitted for a new pair of walking boots.

While strolling through the vegetable market, Alexa slipped her hand into Elizabeth's. These displays of affection were becoming more common, and the little girl told Elizabeth that she hoped she would always be her governess.

"Alexa, I am afraid that is not possible. In a few weeks, Mr. and Mrs. Bingley and I shall be returning to England."

"But Papa and I are to go to England as well! We are to go by a different route, but once we are in England, you will come to Pemberley."

Elizabeth was aware that Mr. Darcy had informed his daughter that they would be returning to England. He had also mentioned that Alexa's reception of the news had been good because she believed Miss Elizabeth would be coming to live with them. In a comment that puzzled her exceedingly, Mr. Darcy had indicated that he had done nothing to correct his daughter, but in Elizabeth's opinion, the misimpression *must* be corrected and the sooner the better.

"I am very pleased that you would want me to serve as your governess, but I am already Cassie's governess. However, Pemberley is close to the manor house that Mr. Bingley is building in Derbyshire, so we shall be able to visit often."

"Papa thinks you would prefer to come to Pemberley." After uttering that statement, Alexa rejoined Cassie who was sampling berries that had just come into the mercato on a farm wagon, but the child's father was soon by her side.

"Miss Elizabeth, you are making it very difficult for me," Mr. Darcy began. "Once I am in England, I must employ a governess for Alexa, and everyone shall pale in comparison with you and what you have accomplished here."

"Children, when treated with kindness, easily transfer their affection. If you choose wisely, Alexa will be welcoming of a new governess. Now that she understands that your absences do not mean that you have left her, she is a most agreeable pupil and eager to learn."

"But the reason she is so agreeable is because my daughter feels safe in your care, which is a good thing, as Bingley and I are to leave for the Palio in two days' time. If Alexa were not so devoted to you, it would not be possible for me to be gone for two days, no less a few weeks. It is very important to me that you and Alexa form a bond. Do you understand what I am saying?"

"Yes, Mr. Darcy," Elizabeth said. "I am quite capable of comprehending the King's English."

Darcy was taken aback by her response. "You find what I have said to be offensive?"

"No, sir, you were not offensive, but you certainly are determined," Elizabeth answered, and then walked ahead of him. Was it absolutely necessary for every conversation to include a discussion of her serving as Alexa's governess? Was there no joy to be had in spending the day with Miss Elizabeth Bennet, formerly of Longbourn Manor, and not Miss Elizabeth, the governess?

Realizing she had been abrupt, if not rude, she soon rejoined him. "Is it an arduous journey to Pistoia?" Elizabeth asked in a calm voice, a calmness she did not feel.

"Actually, no, it is not an arduous journey, that is, if it does not rain. The roads north of Rome are usually in good repair. I was to have gone to Pistoia two years ago, but it was a very wet summer in Tuscany, as well as in France, making travel quite difficult, so much so that it delayed my mother-in-law's arrival at Le Torri Dorate. So some good came out of it," he said in a serious tone. But when he broke into a smile, Elizabeth was completely disarmed.

"I see you share the male trait of making jokes at the expense of their mothers-in-law. My father was very fond of teasing my mother about my grandmother," Elizabeth said, her spirits lifted by the new direction of the conversation. "I think there are few sons-in-law who can resist. It fits the stereotype."

"But stereotypes have their roots in the truth, do they not?"

"In the case of my late grandmother, yes. She was very much a chatterbox, a trait inherited by her daughter and at least two of her granddaughters," Elizabeth said, thinking of Lydia and Kitty.

"Bingley tells me that your father is quite the wit and a good deal of it is at your mother's expense."

"Yes, that is true, but none of us is spared, including dear, sweet Jane. When Jane and Charles announced their betrothal, my father stated that they were both so complying that nothing would ever be resolved on, that every servant would cheat them, and that their generosity would cause them to exceed their income."

"Exceed their income! Not likely with what Bingley's investments bring in!"

"That is very nearly what my mother's response was to my father's comment."

"Your mother and I had similar thoughts? Oh, dear!"

"Mr. Darcy!"

"Of course, I am in jest. But speaking of my departure for Pistoia, I have arranged for Signor and Signora Ciampi to act as your escorts and guides during our absence."

Thinking of Signora Ciampi's appetite for gossip, Elizabeth asked if it was necessary always to be in the company of the notario and his wife when the gentlemen were absent.

"Could we not ask Mario to serve as our escort?" Mario, the eldest son of Signor Moncini, the caretaker of Le Torri Dorate, acted as Mr. Darcy's driver and valet, but Elizabeth knew that he was not to accompany Mr. Darcy to the Palio.

"Absolutely not!" Darcy answered emphatically. "Mario is a good lad, but he is also nineteen and very interested in the ladies. With his mind elsewhere, it would be the same as if you went into Florence without any escort at all."

"Of course, Mario would not be interested in me because I am a spinster," Elizabeth said, teasing.

"You are not a spinster!" Darcy answered with a look of surprise.

"I see you adhere to the definition of a spinster as being eight and twenty, but I am but a few months shy of the mark."

"My definition of a spinster is someone who sits silently in a corner knitting or doing needlepoint or rocking a cradle with her foot," Darcy insisted. "And I know you are teasing me because Mario is a boy, not a man, and you would have no wish to be the object of a boy's attentions."

"I do not think I have to worry about either man or boy, but that is neither here nor there. We were speaking of the Ciampis."

"If you recall, when you first arrived, I warned you about Florence's criminal element which is why I asked the Ciampis to serve as your guides. Because Signor Ciampi's office is very near to the Piazza della Signoria, his confederates are always looking out for you."

"I had no idea," Elizabeth said. This revelation explained the freedom with which Elizabeth and Jane were allowed to move about the piazza and the mercato. Now that she knew of Mr. Darcy's arrangement with Signor Ciampi, she could recall at least a few occasions when she felt as if she was being watched. "I perfectly understand your reasoning, so please allow me to put your mind at ease. While Charles and you are in Pistoia, Jane and I shall not stir from the villa without having made prior arrangements with the signor. You need not worry. I give you my word."

"I appreciate that, and please forgive me if I expressed my opinion too forcefully, but you must understand that I have been in Florence long enough to have heard of numerous assaults on English tourists. Their naiveté and gullibility make them easy prey for villains bent on thievery."

"I truly do understand that you were acting in our best interest."

"I would hope that I should always do so, but in speaking of my departure, is there anything in particular you wish to visit before I leave for Pistoia?"

In the weeks since their arrival, Elizabeth had used her time outside the classroom to visit Florence's famous sites, often accompanied by their host. Even so, she felt that she had not done justice to the Uffizi collection and arrangements were made for Mr. Darcy and Elizabeth to go into Florence.

Standing in front of Fra Filippo Lippi's *Madonna and Child*, Darcy indicated that it was one of his favorite paintings.

"I love it because of that angel," Darcy said, pointing to a winged boy supporting the Christ child. "Because he has been given such an important task, he is quite pleased with himself. In his look, I also detect a hint of mischief."

"Would this be a look familiar to your own nursemaid and governess, Mr. Darcy?" Elizabeth asked.

"I will admit that as a boy I got into a fair amount of mischief."

"I am surprised to hear it. When I was at Pemberley, your gardener sang your praises."

"Would you expect otherwise? I am the one who pays him."

Their next stop was in front of a painting of Federico, Duke of Urbino, dressed in full armor, who was kneeling in front of the Virgin Mary. Elizabeth declared that with the duke off to the far right, the picture looked unbalanced.

"It is unbalanced," Darcy said. "The open area to the left was intended for Battista Sforza, Federico's duchess, who had died. I believe the space was deliberately left empty as a way for the duke to share his grief and to tell the world that no one could ever take the place of his beloved wife."

Elizabeth gently placed her hand on the sleeve of Mr. Darcy's coat. "I can imagine what you are thinking."

Although Darcy looked directly at her, it was as if he was seeing through her. "If you could read my mind, Miss Elizabeth, I think you would be surprised at what you would find there." And he placed his hand over hers.

Chapter 19

With the men away at the Palio, Elizabeth was spending more time with the children in the classroom and less time on excursions into Florence. Neither Cassie nor Alexa was complaining, but Cassie's mother was.

"When we first came to Florence, you said that we would only spend three days a week in the classroom," Jane said, "but today is the fourth day of lessons."

"It is because of the heat," Elizabeth answered, pulling her frock away from her skin. "Just traveling into Florence is fatiguing. By the time I get out of the carriage, I am already drenched in sweat. The other day, when I was in the Medici Chapel, I slipped off my shoes so that I could feel the cool of the marble floor."

"Is there a reason other than the heat that keeps you at Le Torri Dorate?"

Because all forays into Florence required coordination with the Ciampis, Elizabeth's enthusiasm for visiting the sights had waned with the departure of Charles and Mr. Darcy. Although she had no quarrel with Signor Ciampi, his wife was another matter.

"You know there is," Elizabeth said in a whisper so that the children would not hear her, and then directed Jane to step out into the garden. "Signora Ciampi is a woman who delights in exposing the most private affairs of people who have somehow offended her. I have yet to meet the British Consul, but when I do, I shall look upon him as a man who keeps a mistress, possibly two, here in Italy whilst his wife remains in England."

An even greater source of irritation was the signora's comments about the late Mrs. Darcy. On several occasions, the wife of the notario had insinuated that the lady's illnesses were all in her head, stating that Mrs. Darcy always rallied whenever her mother and sister were in Florence, only to take to her bed as soon as the visit had ended. Jane had attempted to defend Amelie Darcy by mentioning her own health problems and the bouts of fatigue that had plagued her. Unfortunately, Signora Ciampi was less charitable in responding, and in Elizabeth's opinion, exposed the true source of her antipathy to Mr. Darcy's wife:

"Mrs. Darcy's preference was to spend most of her time with members of the French community, holdovers from a time when Napoleon's sister Elisa had been named grand duchess of Tuscany," Signora Ciampi had complained. *"The guest list for her soirees was limited to these chosen few. Although she was in good enough health to host such gatherings, when an invitation came from a fellow Englishman, she was always indisposed."*

"Is it not obvious that Signora Ciampi's dislike of Mrs. Darcy is a result of her being excluded from Mrs. Darcy's entertainments?" Elizabeth asked.

"With the men in Pistoia, we cannot go into Florence without Signor Ciampi, and, apparently, the husband will not go without the wife. Signora Ciampi is a means to an end."

"Jane, all pleasure in being in Florence falls away when I am in that woman's company. I would rather remain here."

"Is it possible that you do not wish to go into Florence unless you are in the company of Mr. Darcy?"

"Jane, whatever do you mean!" a shocked Elizabeth asked too loudly.

Jane put her finger to her lips. After returning to the cellar where Cassie and Alexa were pretending to study, Jane dismissed the children for the afternoon.

"Let us stay in here, Lizzy. It is too hot outside for any discussion."

Stepping into the classroom, Elizabeth inhaled the earthy smell of the former root cellar, reminding her of Longbourn when the ploughmen were preparing the soil for spring planting, and for a moment, she longed for home and the company of her family. Elizabeth sat down on a bench, her head resting against the cool of the cellar's stucco walls.

Jane joined her sister on the bench and took hold of her hand. "Lizzy, the reason why you do not want to go into Florence is because you wish to see these wonderful works of art with Mr. Darcy," a statement Elizabeth did not challenge. "When you told me of your regret in refusing Mr. Darcy, I assumed you were speaking of being deprived of the tangible benefits that came with being the wife of a man of substance. By marrying Mr. Darcy, you would have been assured of a comfortable life with a man you could respect, if not love. But in our weeks here at Le Torri Dorate, I have been watching you, and I have come to realize that you have fallen in love with Mr. Darcy. Tell me if I am wrong."

For a few minutes, Elizabeth sat in silence allowing the stillness of the room to enter her very being. If anyone other than Jane had been aware of her feelings for Mr. Darcy, she would have been mortified, but Jane was more than a sister; she was Elizabeth's dearest friend. And she was relieved to have it out in the open as it allowed her to speak of her love for Mr. Darcy, feelings that had overwhelmed her when the Master of Pemberley had first taken her hand in Livorno.

"No, you are not wrong. Until I came here, I had no idea of the depth of my feelings for Mr. Darcy. Despite your excellent company and the presence of the children, I find I am terribly lonely."

With tears forming, Elizabeth thought of the wonderful times she had spent in Mr. Darcy's company. There was one particular day when they had walked arm-in-arm along the Ponte alle Grazie, a promenade that paralleled the Arno, and a passerby had addressed them as Signor and Signora, and for a moment, she had pretended that they were, in fact, Mr. and Mrs. Darcy, and they were visiting Florence as a part of their honeymoon journey.

With the rays of the sun infusing the river with brilliant light, they had dined at a riverside *ristorante* where they spoke of many things, but mostly of England and home. Mr. Darcy had been eager to share with Elizabeth his plans for Pemberley. The manor house, which was nearly a hundred years old, was in need of renovation. The kitchen was hopelessly out-of-date for the entertainments he planned, and because his mother's apartments were decades out of fashion, they were in desperate need of attention. When Elizabeth had asked him if it would not be best to leave such extensive alterations to the mistress's apartment to its future occupant, he indicated that those were his plans exactly. "Any changes must reflect my wife's wishes and sense of style."

Elizabeth remembered thinking how fortunate the second Mrs. Darcy would be.

The day had ended at their favorite place in all of Florence, the entrance to the Duomo, where a man was playing a romantic ballad on a violin. As a reward for his excellent performance, Mr. Darcy had taken Elizabeth's hand and had gently opened it. After placing a coin in it, he had gestured for her to toss it into the open case of the instrument. With his thumb resting on her wrist just above her glove, she felt her pulse accelerate, his touch sending a charge through her unlike anything she had ever felt before.

During the carriage ride to the villa, Elizabeth had imagined Mr. Darcy taking her into his arms and kissing her, a scene she recreated in her mind nearly every night before drifting off to sleep. But there would be no kisses on that night or any other. Once she stepped onto the gravel drive, the reality of her position at Le Torri Dorate, that of governess to her niece and Mr. Darcy's daughter, reasserted itself.

"I am feeling rather guilty, Lizzy. I believe you refused Mr. Darcy because he was instrumental in separating Charles and me."

Elizabeth looked surprised. She had never shared that part of Mr. Darcy's letter in which he had admitted his role in their separation.

"I learned of it from Caroline. Fearing that I would dislike her and Louisa for the role they had played, she was quick to blame Mr. Darcy. Although I pretended to accept her explanation, I did not believe Mr. Darcy had acted alone."

"And by that time, you had come to know the real Caroline Bingley and Louisa Hurst."

Jane nodded. She could hardly reconcile the mean-spiritedness of Caroline and Louisa before her marriage to Charles with the fawning relations who had visited her so frequently at Netherfield Park and in Derby.

"Rather than dwell on the only time in our lives when Charles and I were unhappy, I chose to banish the unfortunate incident from my mind. To everyone involved, all has been forgiven, and I hope you will forgive me as well."

"Jane, please do not blame yourself. Mr. Darcy's interference was only one reason for my refusal. His supposed mistreatment of George Wickham played a greater role in my decision." Lizzy blushed at the memory of how she had believed Wickham's lies to the detriment of Mr. Darcy. "There were other provocations as well: his arrogance, for one. I particularly remember a conversation in which he admitted that his opinion once lost was lost forever. Because of such statements, I thought of him as cold and unfeeling, and I judged him too harshly."

"I am not sure that you did misjudge him, Lizzy. He *was* rude; he *was* above his company. But he is a different man now. Your rejection chastened him, and because of your rebuke, he has changed."

"Dear Jane, you give me too much credit. I think he changed by virtue of becoming a husband and a father. The love of his wife and child altered him greatly, and he is a better man because of them."

"We can debate the reasons for Mr. Darcy's transformation, but that does not help you. What is to be done, Lizzy?"

"Nothing. There is nothing to be done. Well, actually, there is something," Elizabeth said, wiping away her tears. "I must stop pouting and make the best use of my time here in Florence as the days go by so quickly. Before you know it, we shall be packing our trunks for our return to England. Which reminds me, if we are to go to Bagno Vignoli, we must do so immediately after the reception at the Consulate or we will be too late."

"I am not going to Bagno Vignoni."

This was the first Elizabeth was hearing of it, and she asked when Jane had made her decision.

"It may sound strange, but it was when I met the *Venus d' Medici*."

After the first encounter with the statue, every subsequent visit to Florence required a side trip to the Tribuna so that Jane might view the goddess of love. Although aware of the effect the statue had had on Jane, Elizabeth attributed her interest to be an admiration for an artistic marvel from the ancient world. She had been unaware of the effect it had had on Jane's emotions.

"I was deeply touched by the look on *Venus's* face," Jane began. "I understood her feelings of apprehension because that is the way I have felt since giving birth to Cassandra."

Elizabeth knew her niece's delivery had been a physical and emotional trauma for Jane, one that had very nearly cost her sister her life. After two days of excruciating labor, the doctors had used forceps to reposition Cassie. Unfortunately, in doing so, the physician had caused a tear, and the blood loss had been considerable. Succeeding months found Jane so weak that she rarely stirred from her bed. Her emotional health took even longer to recover.

"Since coming to Florence, I have had time to examine my role as Charles's wife," she said, turning to Elizabeth so that she was looking directly at her. "You do know that there is only way to prevent the conception of a child, do you not?"

"It is necessary to remain chaste."

"I am not referring to how a maiden prevents the loss of her virtue," Jane said, smiling, "but how a married woman avoids conception. There is only one way: abstinence. Although the times when Charles and I came together as man and wife were infrequent, my dear, sweet husband made no objection because he, too, feared a second pregnancy. Things changed whilst we were in Paris when Charles was made aware of something a man can use to prevent a woman from becoming pregnant. As a result, we have enjoyed…"

"I understand," Elizabeth said, blushing. "All is well with Mr. and Mrs. Bingley behind closed doors."

"But all these changes came about as a result of the *Venus d' Medici*. I wanted to be reborn, and most particularly, to stop being an invalid. I am not yet thirty years old, but I have been acting as if I am in my dotage. Since my encounter with *Venus*, I have improved every day, and I am convinced my cure would not have happened if I had not come to Florence. In England, our society demands that all of our emotions be turned inward, but here in Italy, all emotions are worn on one's sleeves. Truthfully, I prefer my feelings to be laid bare, come what may."

"My goodness, Jane, that is quite a change!"

"And a change for the better. If I had not been so fearful of the criticism of others, if I had been more open about my feelings for Charles when he first came to Hertfordshire, no one, not even the imperious Mr. Darcy, would have been able to take him away from me. I have learned a lot from that experience. My timidity has been replaced with forthrightness. I highly recommend it."

"If you are saying that I should throw myself at Mr. Darcy, I can assure you that I would do so if I thought for one minute that he would be there to catch me," Elizabeth said only half in jest. "But my time has passed."

"Are you sure?"

"Absolutely. Mr. Darcy has mentioned several times that it is his intention to look for a wife once he is in England and is already making plans for improvements to her apartment at Pemberley. Another thing he frequently mentions is how happy Miss Darcy is to have me as her governess, and Alexa has brought up the subject as well. I think before leaving Florence Mr. Darcy will ask me to serve in that position, at least until a suitable governess can be found, and I can tell you that I am dreading the moment."

"Then make sure it does not happen." Elizabeth laughed at her sister's remark. "Let me be clearer. If you are once again to capture Mr. Darcy's heart, you must let him know that you wish to be more than Alexa's governess; you wish to be his wife. In that regard, you must make the most of the time that is left to you."

"And what am I supposed to do to advance my cause? Shall I disregard convention and write him letters? Wet down my muslin dress so that Mr. Darcy might better admire my figure?" Elizabeth said, trying to make light of a serious situation.

"You are being ridiculous, Lizzy," Jane said, dismissing Lizzy's suggestions. "When I say that you must find a way to let Mr. Darcy know of your feelings, I am being quite serious, and you must be serious as well."

All that was well and good in theory, but what Jane was suggesting would require a transformation of her very being. Even at twenty, Elizabeth had not been flirtatious. If she had attracted the attention of a gentleman, it had been the result of a combination of intelligence and wit. It was certainly not because of her beauty. Even Mr. Darcy had declared her to be only tolerable. It seemed unlikely that at nearly eight and twenty, she was capable of undergoing so radical a change to her personality. On the other hand, Jane was right; her time with Mr. Darcy was drawing to a close. If she did not act now, she would not have another chance. With her mind racing, she thought of another obstacle.

"Jane, is it possible Mr. Darcy is still angry with me for my refusal of his offer, and that by asking me to be Alexa's governess, he has been presented with an opportunity to embarrass me? After all, I did embarrass *him*."

Jane shook her head. "If it was Mr. Darcy's intention to exact some form of retribution, he had his opportunity to do so when he learned of Lydia and Wickham's disgraceful exit from Brighton. Instead of celebrating our discomfort, he did all that he could to alleviate it."

Elizabeth had to agree, and she thought how difficult it must have been for Mr. Darcy to negotiate with a man who had tried to seduce his own sister. And why had Mr. Darcy intervened? The answer to that question had to be that at the time of Lydia's elopement, he was still in love with her. With that knowledge, Elizabeth resolved to try, as her mother would say, "to get" Mr. Darcy.

"Charlotte once told me that in order for a woman to secure the affection of a man, she had better show more affection than she feels."

"I disagree with that statement," Jane answered. "I think it is important that a relationship be based on honesty. You should show no more, and no less, than what you feel."

Before speaking, Elizabeth wiped tears from her eyes. "In any event, I am unable to follow Charlotte's advice as it is impossible for me to love Mr. Darcy any more than I already do."

Chapter 20

When they first arrived at Le Torri Dorate, Cassie and Elizabeth were to have shared a bedroom, and to that end, Cassie's trunk had been delivered to Elizabeth's bedchamber. In a moment, all that had changed when Alexa invited Cassie to stay with her in her own room. Over time, with the exception of a collection of stories that Elizabeth read to the children at bedtime, everything that belonged to Cassie Bingley had migrated to Alexa's room.

On a stormy night, with shutters rattling and pots moving on their own across the terrace, Elizabeth invited the frightened children to sleep with her in her giant canopied bed. Because Cassie and Alexa had heard all of the tales in Elizabeth's storybook, they asked if they could make up their own. Tonight it was Alexa's turn.

Once upon a time, there was a beautiful lady with golden hair who lived in a beautiful house in the hills above Florence. The lady was married to a handsome prince who granted her every wish. The prince and

princess had a little girl, and they loved her and bought
her many pretty things from the mercato.

"What is the little girl's name?" Elizabeth asked,
amused by the transparency of the identity of the prince
and his family.

After giving it some thought, Alexa decided on
Beatrice.

While her Mama stayed at the house, Beatrice and
her dear Papa would go for pony rides in the hills. He
would take her for carriage rides, and when it was very
hot, he allowed her to put her feet into the fountain in
the garden.

When they got home, they would always visit Mama,
who was sleeping in her bed. When she awoke, Mama
would read to Beatrice from a book that was trimmed in
gold until night came. Papa would come to say good
night and to tell them how much he loved them. Before
going to his own room, he would always tell Beatrice
what they would do the next day and that is what
Beatrice would dream about. The End.

"Well, Beatrice was very fortunate to have such
loving parents, and ones who bought her pretty gifts
from the shops," Elizabeth said, tweaking the child's
chin.

"But they did not live happily ever after," the real
Beatrice answered.

"Why is that?"

"Because the princess died, and the prince and
Beatrice were very sad."

"Why did the princess die?" Cassie asked.

"Papa said she had a fliction."

"An affliction," Elizabeth said, correcting her, and she placed her arms around the two girls and pulled them close to her. This was the first time Alexa had made any reference to the passing of her mother, and Elizabeth wondered if Cassie even knew what it meant to have someone die.

"Although it is sad that the princess died, we can take comfort in knowing that she is in heaven with God and his angels."

"That is what Papa says," Alexa answered. "The angels came and took Mama to heaven where she lives happily in the clouds."

Cassie frowned. "I do not want angels to take *my* mama, and I do not want to live in the clouds. That is where the storms are."

"Heaven is far above the storm clouds, Cassie," her Aunt Elizabeth reassured her, "and you have no reason to fear that your mama will be taken from you."

"But why was Alexa's mother taken away?"

Elizabeth did not know what to say. Without speaking to Mr. Darcy, she was reluctant to talk about Mrs. Darcy's passing. Had he discussed with Alexa that his wife was now in the presence of God? And how was that presence described?

"One day, each of us will have a home in heaven, and it is God who will decide when to call us into his presence." But that was all that she was prepared to say on that subject. "Alexa, I know that for the last week of your mother's life that she was confined to bed, but that was not always the case."

Apparently, with her mother gone for more than a year, the memories of their time together were slipping away to be replaced by the final days of her life, a time when Amelie Darcy was suffering from the effects of influenza.

"If you look about this room and other rooms in the villa, you will find many of your mother's paintings. In her watercolors, I recognize the fountain in the garden and the villa across the valley. There are drawings of the Duomo and the campanile. Your mother would have been in the garden or on the front lawn when she painted these scenes. I think tomorrow we should look at each one. I am sure they will spark a memory." Alexa made no comment. "And we shall do something fun tomorrow. Is that agreeable?"

Both girls nodded enthusiastically.

"May Cassie and I go riding?" Alexa asked. "With Signor Roberto away, I have not seen my pony, but the signor is now at Palazzo Bardi."

Elizabeth had been advised by Mr. Darcy that Alexa's pony was stabled at Count Bardi's stables on an adjacent property and that he had given his permission for Alexa to ride once the count had returned to his villa from his travels in the north.

"How do you know Signor Roberto has come back to Palazzo Bardi?"

"Mario told me. Signora Parisi is Mario's aunt."

"And who is Signora Parisi?"

"Signora Parisi is Signor Roberto's housekeeper. She is the sister of Signora Moncini and Signor Ciampi."

"What! Mario Moncini is related to Signor Ciampi? Why did I not know this?"

Alexa shrugged.

Elizabeth thought about all the Moncinis who worked on the estate. There were Moncinis everywhere, and they came in all shapes and sizes and with varying degrees of responsibility. In addition to Signor and Signora Moncini, there was Flora, their eldest daughter, who acted as nursery maid, and Mario, who served as valet to Mr. Darcy and Charles, as well as numerous sons, daughters, nieces, and nephews. And every one of them was related to Signora Ciampi by marriage.

Elizabeth found this news startling, and it explained so much. If the Moncinis and Ciampis were related, then it was obvious how news of Mrs. Darcy's comings and goings at the villa had reached the ears of Signora Ciampi in Florence.

An unsettled Elizabeth indicated that she would send Mario with a message to Palazzo Bardi to ask, weather permitting, if they might ride. "Alexa, I shall need you to interpret."

Alexa shook her head. "Mario speaks English." Elizabeth's eyes went wide. "Flora also speaks English, but not nearly as well as Mario. They went to the English language school near San Lorenzo."

"We shall speak of this again in the morning. It is time to turn down the lamp." After extinguishing the flame, she sang a lullaby. In a few minutes, despite the storm, the children were asleep, and Elizabeth quickly made her way down the hallway to Jane's room where she found her sister at her writing desk.

"Am I disturbing you?" Elizabeth asked.

"Of course not," Jane said, placing her pen in the inkwell. "I was writing letters, one to Kitty and a second to Mama. I have also been remiss in responding to Caroline's last letter."

"I feel guilty that I have not written to Kitty to acknowledge her news, and I owe Mama and Papa a letter." She had nothing to say about Caroline who, having married a baronet, was even more obnoxious than when Elizabeth had first met her in Meryton.

"As a mother, it makes sense for me to write to Kitty as she had a few questions, but from her last letter, I can say that this pregnancy is going a lot more smoothly than the first. As to our parents, we agreed that we would take turns, and it is my turn to write. In truth, you are always busy with Cassie and Alexa, and because you are here, I assume the children are already asleep." Elizabeth nodded. "I am surprised to hear it as Cassie is afraid of thunder and lightning."

"I shall warn you that when you next see your daughter, you may find that she is fearful of something else." Elizabeth related Cassie's concerns that her mother might be taken from her as Alexa's mother had been. "I tried to reassure her, but as Mr. Darcy once said to me, 'How do you explain death to a child?' But that is not why I have come."

Elizabeth informed Jane of the relationship between the Moncinis and Ciampis. After thinking about it for a moment, Jane shrugged.

"Don't you see, Jane? The Moncinis, and Mario and Flora in particular, would be in a position to hear conversations between Mr. and Mrs. Darcy. Even if their understanding of English is imperfect, any elevation in voices would have revealed much."

"I am sorry, Lizzy, but I still do not see the problem."

"It is not a problem for us, but it explains how Signora Ciampi knew so much about Mrs. Darcy. I am sure that woman did not hesitate to ask her husband's nephew and niece about the private affairs of the family."

Jane agreed with her sister's assessment, but insisted that if any harm had been done, it had been buried with Mrs. Darcy in Livorno.

Elizabeth was surprised that Jane was not as unnerved as she was. If she had been aware that Mario and Flora understood English, she would have been more guarded when speaking to her sister, but there was another matter of equal concern: Mrs. Darcy's passing.

"Alexa's memories of her mother are fading, and for some reason, I feel it is my responsibility to remind her about her mother."

"Why would you do such a thing?" Jane asked, her raised eyebrows indicating her surprise. "If it is your plan to rekindle the flame with Mr. Darcy, reminding him of his wife may not be the best way to go about it."

"Jane, I must confess that Mr. Darcy's relationship with his wife puzzles me exceedingly," her statement punctuated by a furrowed brow. "He speaks of her in such ambiguous terms that I cannot draw a picture of her in my mind. One minute I am convinced that no one can take her place, and in the next, Mr. Darcy mentions making changes to Pemberley for the benefit of a second Mrs. Darcy. I cannot make it out. You met Mrs. Darcy. What do you think?"

Jane had little to add to what was already known of Amelie Darcy. When the couple had stayed at Netherfield Park, it had only been for four short days as Mrs. Darcy was eager to rejoin friends in London, and Jane reminded her sister that at the time of the Darcys' visit, she was still recovering from Cassie's birth.

"Mrs. Darcy understood that it was necessary for me to rest frequently, and she said that she was perfectly capable of amusing herself." Looking at Lizzy, Jane could see that her answer did not satisfy, and she dug deeper. "Mrs. Darcy did say that being a married man had not changed Mr. Darcy."

"What did she mean by that?"

"That her husband remained of a taciturn nature. With the exception of his devotion to his daughter, he was not one to show his emotions. She said she was rather like him in that regard. I took it to mean that she kept her own counsel—that she was not one to share her feelings with her husband."

Jane's remarks only added to Lizzy's confusion. "In four days, that is the only thing of a personal nature Mrs. Darcy uttered—that her husband was of a taciturn nature?"

Jane went quiet trying to resurrect distant memories, but there was not all that much to dig up. Rather than play cards, where conversation would have been possible, the lady's preference was to play the pianoforte. When told of a dance to be held at the assembly hall, Mrs. Darcy had stated that although her health did not permit her to dance, Mr. Darcy need not stay at Netherfield on her account, but he would not go without her.

"However, of one thing I am sure," Jane said, "Mrs. Darcy was a great reader."

Jane's statement sparked a memory of her own: a conversation with Caroline Bingley about what constituted an accomplished lady. To Caroline's long list, Mr. Darcy had added that reading books was of equal importance to singing, painting tables, and being fluent in a modern language.

If Mrs. Darcy improved her mind through extensive reading, then that alone would have drawn him to Amelie Cantwell.

"What was discussed during supper?" Elizabeth asked. "Surely the lady could not avoid conversation when only the four of you were at table."

"Oh, Lizzy, I can hardly remember what I said and did yesterday, and those suppers were so long ago." Under Lizzy's steady gaze, Jane continued to dredge for memories. "Ah, yes! Mrs. Darcy spoke extensively of Spa. She was very fond of its little theater and outdoor musicals. She was also very enthusiastic about her time in Paris as she had a keen interest in fashion."

"Did she mention Pemberley?"

"Yes, she said she found English weather to be too wet for her taste and that Derbyshire had even more rain than London. I do remember remarking on how keen our husbands were about horses and riding—that they were often gone for hours at a time. I mentioned that I wished my riding skills were better so that I might join Charles. But Mrs. Darcy said she had no intention of learning to ride. By her statement, I took it to mean that she did not ride at all. Even so, she had no objection to Mr. Darcy riding as much as he pleased. While the men were away, she either read or did needlepoint. That is all I can tell you."

"Jane, you bring me thin gruel," a distressed Elizabeth said. "I now regret that I returned to Longbourn during their visit, but to be in such close proximity to Mr. Darcy after the words we had exchanged at Hunsford, I had not the courage to remain."

"Well, you have met the lady. What did *you* think of Mrs. Darcy?"

"If you recall, I was but one of a large party, and Mama talked incessantly."

She remembered her mother advising Mrs. Darcy, who was wearing an exquisite ivory silk dress, where the best warehouses were to be found in London. The lady, who would have had her own dressmaker, made no comment. During supper, Elizabeth had chosen a seat at the opposite end of the table to Mrs. Darcy, her regret in refusing Mr. Darcy causing her to keep her distance from the woman who had accepted his proposal.

But this examination of Jane was getting her nowhere. "Never mind about Mrs. Darcy. We were speaking of Alexa. I feel quite strongly that I must do all that I can to make sure that the memories of her mother are not extinguished. Tomorrow, I want to visit those parts of the garden where her mother sketched or painted. Hopefully that will resurrect memories of Mrs. Darcy for Alexa."

"Lizzy, of course you must do what you think is best. But, I believe, Alexa's preference would be to ride her pony. We shall see in the morning."

Chapter 21

The result of the previous night's storm had been a drop in temperatures from tropical into the comfortable range, and it was a delightful morning. After first viewing Mrs. Darcy's sketches, it had been Elizabeth's intention to spend the day in the garden locating the sites depicted in the drawings, but her plan immediately went awry.

"You were right, Jane," Elizabeth said, collapsing into a chair on the terrace. At breakfast, all Alexa and Cassie talked about was visiting Signor Roberto so that they could ride the ponies. The only way I could get them to speak of other things was to promise to send Mario with a note for Count Bardi asking if we might visit tomorrow."

"Asking the children to choose between a walk in a garden that they have been exploring for weeks and riding ponies, well, Lizzy, you gave yourself an impossible task. If you were in their shoes, which would you choose?"

Jane was right. What child would pass up the chance to ride a pony? At this point, she would not mind riding a sturdy horse in the hills surrounding Le Torri Dorate or taking a long walk along its many paths, especially if she were in the company of Mr. Darcy, and she recalled the many occasions Mr. Darcy had joined in her perambulations about Rosings Park.

At the time, she had felt all the perverseness of meeting him. To prevent it from happening again, she had taken care to inform him that this particular path was a favorite haunt of hers and one she visited daily. With such a direct warning, she did not understand how their meeting had occurred a second time and even a third. It seemed like willful ill-nature or a voluntary penance because on these occasions, Mr. Darcy actually thought it necessary to walk with her! He never said a great deal, but it struck her in the course of their third encounter that he was asking some unconnected questions about her enjoyment of Mrs. Collins's company or the beauty of the grounds. In speaking of the manor house, he seemed to expect that whenever she came into Kent again that she would be staying *there* too. At the time, she had thought he might have had Colonel Fitzwilliam in mind for her as that gentleman had shown some interest, but that had not been the case.

He was speaking of me visiting Rosings as his wife! How obtuse can one be! And to think I might have been presented to Lady Catherine as her niece! I am sure she would have thrown a vase at me. No, not a vase, a piece of crockery—something used by the servants.

Elizabeth shook the memory from her mind because the pain of the recollection was greater than her enjoyment of picturing crockery in flight at Rosings Park.

"While awaiting Count Bardi's response to my note, it is my intention to adhere to my plan and view Mrs. Darcy's drawings and paintings with the children. I hope that for Alexa they will resurrect memories of her mother."

Elizabeth began the tour in the drawing room where several of Mrs. Darcy's watercolors were on display. After discussing technique and the choice of color, the children were encouraged to tell a story about each scene. While viewing a lovely crayon sketch of the Duomo, Cassie delighted her mother and aunt with a tale about a little girl dancing round and round on its tiled roof. Upon reaching the very peak of the lantern, she became an angel and flew away.

Alexa was less forthcoming, and the first four paintings brought little response. It was the fifth, a watercolor featuring the fountain at the heart of the garden, that shook loose some memories.

"While I walked around the base of the fountain, Mama would hold my hand," Alexa began. "Unlike Papa, she would not let me put my feet in the water because there were fish in there, and she told me that they would nibble on my toes. I thought I should like that, but Mama said, 'What if they nibble them until there is nothing left?' I thought that was funny that I should have no toes and wondered how I would walk."

Any further viewing was postponed when Signor Moncini announced that Count Bardi had arrived at Le Torri Dorate, and the children were allowed to follow their favorite activity: the pursuit of the estate's many cats and kittens. As soon as the man was free of his carriage, the count, a tall, slender man in his late fifties, bounded into the villa. After introductions were made, he kissed the hands of the two ladies and then apologized for not visiting sooner.

"My most profuse apologies. I only arrived at my villa two days ago. Because I have been gone for so long, I had many letters to write, but I should have sent a note telling you of my return." He immediately offered the full use of his stables. "Do you ride, Mrs. Bingley?"

"I do, sir, but not for pleasure, much to the disappointment of my husband."

"It was the same with my wife," he said, sighing. "The contessa found sitting in a saddle to be uncomfortable." The count shifted his hips back and forth as a way to demonstrate his wife's particular grievance with sitting on a horse. "Despite my love of horses and her lack of enthusiasm, we were happily married for twenty-five years until her passing five years ago. And you, Miss Elizabeth? Do you ride?"

"I do, sir. Although my riding skills are merely adequate, I do so with great pleasure. When I am at home in England, I often ride with my brother-in-law, Mr. Bingley."

"I had the pleasure of riding with Bingley earlier in the week in Pistoia. I agree Bingley's skills *are* excellent, and he is quite fearless, a necessity if you are to truly enjoy such a spirited animal."

"Are Charles and Mr. Darcy still in Pistoia?" Jane asked. Since she had not had a letter from Charles in the past three days, she suspected he was on his way to Fiesole, which the count confirmed.

"I can tell you that Darcy and Bingley are now enjoying the trails that wind their way through the hills above Fiesole. From there, you get a bird's-eye view of Florence. It is quite spectacular, but you must be an accomplished equestrian so that your mount will feel confident going up such steep trails. If your horse does not trust you, you could move heaven and earth, and he will not budge!"

"Count Bardi, there is no reason for us to stand in the foyer," Jane said. "Will you please join us for tea on the terrace?"

"With pleasure."

They had only just sat down when a Moncini daughter appeared with a tray holding a pitcher full of tea and a plate full of sliced lemons. After squeezing the juice of the lemon into his glass, the count spoke of the bumper crop of lemons that his estate was producing. Pointing to the pulp floating in his glass, he mentioned that his wife used to refer to them as "the tears of the Madonna."

"What a lovely allusion," Elizabeth said.

"Yes, with my wife, because Mary was her patron saint, everything was about the Virgin. We have a chapel on my estate that is dedicated to her. But what would you expect living in a city with the Duomo dedicated to the Mother of God?"

The count was full of news about Pistoia, and he described in detail the race for the *palio*, explaining that at one time, before the advent of the mechanical loom had lowered the price of textiles, the cloth bestowed on the winner had been quite valuable and could be sold for a small fortune.

"With your men away, how have you been amusing yourselves?" Bardi asked.

"Because of the heat, we have been spending most of our time here at the villa enjoying the gardens," Jane answered. "We have only gone into Florence twice."

"Yes, the heat. It can be oppressive, and I agree, it is much cooler up here in the hills. But why did you restrict yourselves to the gardens at Le Torri Dorate? I may sound as if I am bragging, but I am telling you the truth when I say that Palazzo Bardi is the largest estate on this ridge, and it has served as a retreat for my family, the Donatis and the Bardis, since the 14th Century. If you had taken a tour of the garden, the head gardener, who speaks something resembling English, would have told you the story of Constanza Donati, the beautiful daughter of Federico Donati, and her lover."

After the count had finished the familiar and much embellished tale, Elizabeth informed him that they had been told that the Buondelmonte/Donati romance had taken place at Le Torri Dorate.

"So Darcy will claim my story! Well, let him try," the count said, laughing. "It is true that Le Torri Dorate *was* owned by the Donati family, but so was every other house on this ridge. These villas were built for two reasons: to escape the heat of Florence and to show off how much money a family had. No one would have been impressed with so small a palazzo as Le Torri Dorate. If memory serves, it was a wedding present given to one of the Donati sons."

So small a palazzo! This statement surprised Elizabeth as she considered the villa to be quite large for a summer residence.

"But in all fairness to Darcy, every family hereabouts claims this story as their own."

"Is there any truth to it?" Elizabeth asked. "Did Constanza go to live in a convent?"

Bardi nodded. "But not for long." He explained that daughters were commodities to be traded amongst Florence's most powerful families, and one did not hide such a jewel in a convent. "After Buondelmonte's assassination, Constanza's father waited for the heat to go out of the fire and then offered Constanza to another son of the Amidei. As you can imagine, it was not a happy marriage. Her husband, believing she pined for Angelo Buondelmonte, never trusted her. After she gave him three sons, he sent her into the country."

"How sad!" Jane exclaimed.

"Oh, but she had her revenge. She outlived her husband by twenty years! There are other stories I could share," he said, rising, "but I do not wish to intrude any longer than I have. But here is what I propose. You will come to my villa for supper this evening. While we enjoy good food and conversation, the children will ride their ponies while the weather is still cool."

"Count Bardi, it is not necessary to entertain us. We..."

"Please allow me to interrupt, Mrs. Bingley. You will be doing me a favor. Between business and the Palio, I have been exclusively in the company of men, and I am a man who craves female companionship. Without women to soften the edges, life would not be worth living."

"Are you sure?" Elizabeth asked. Despite Mr. Darcy's approval of such an excursion, she did not know the count.

Bardi laughed. "You are a mother hen protecting her chick. It is just as Mr. Darcy had hoped. In his absence, he was eager to have you and Alexa enjoy each other's company."

Elizabeth looked to Jane. Here was another instance of Mr. Darcy viewing her exclusively as his daughter's governess.

"You have nothing to worry about as Alexa and her young friend will be under the watchful eye of my stable master," Count Bardi continued. "Antonio is an accomplished equestrian. In fact, he won the Palio here in Florence three times before retiring. There is no better trainer in the whole of Tuscany."

After agreeing to the count's plan, Elizabeth and Jane walked with the gentleman to the entrance of the villa where his carriage awaited.

"You are both so lovely. I do not understand how your men can stay away so long. I would have rushed home from Pistoia."

Although Jane smiled at the compliment, Elizabeth blushed. "Count Bardi, Mr. Darcy is not *my man*. I am here at Le Torri Dorate because of my relationship to Mrs. Bingley."

"Really? Then I must have misunderstood." After bowing, he climbed into his carriage. "I shall send my carriage at five o'clock this evening. That will give the children ample time to ride before the sun sets."

When Jane nodded, the count signaled for the driver to proceed.

After seeing the carriage well down the drive, Jane asked Elizabeth what she thought about the count referring to her as Mr. Darcy's woman.

"In a broad sense, I *am* Mr. Darcy's woman," Elizabeth answered. "I have agreed to serve as Alexa's governess, and, as such, I am in his employ."

"Hmm" was all Jane would say.

Chapter 22

Looking for the perfect dress to wear to supper at Palazzo Bardi, Jane scanned the contents of a wardrobe bulging with the purchases she had made in Paris. Even though there were few colors that did not compliment her fair complexion, yellow remained her best color. So it was no surprise when Jane selected a pale yellow dress with scalloping on the sleeves and two tiers of rosettes on the hem. A visit with the count was the closest the two ladies had come to an evening's entertainment outside Le Torri Dorate since their arrival, and they must look their best.

While Jane was all about frills and flounces, Elizabeth preferred the simpler styles she had worn when she had first come out into society. From her time in Paris, she knew that if London followed Paris's lead, with its wider skirts and puffy sleeves, when she returned home, she would be out of style. With no one to notice, did it really matter?

After eyeing her own array of dresses, Elizabeth chose the pale rose that Jane had commissioned for her sister from her favorite *modiste* in Paris. Her two young charges, who were propped up on her bed, approved of her selection and encouraged her to hurry so that they might spend more time on their ponies. Because Cassie was quite the little rider, she was as eager as Alexa to go to Palazzo Bardi.

The closeness of the girls reminded Elizabeth of her own childhood at Longbourn, a time of general prosperity on the farm, when long summer days had been spent on horseback or walking along the streams that bisected the farms of Hertfordshire. In his latest letter, Papa had written that things were definitely improving. For the first time in four years, he had managed to sell all of his corn, and after breeding two pairs of Gritstone sheep, gifts from Mr. Bingley, he found the amount of wool produced was excellent. Not only was theirs a superior fleece, but it brought a higher selling price on the domestic market. That was the good news.

The bad news was that Lydia was once again at Longbourn and expecting her fourth child. Unlike previous visits that followed a quarrel between Mr. and Mrs. Wickham, this separation would not end in a reconciliation and a return to Newcastle. With no wars to fight, Wickham's regiment had been disbanded, and George Wickham was no longer an officer. With no prospects for employment, he had turned his wrath on his wife, and she had fled to Longbourn.

Lizzy understood that with Lydia's arrival, the house would be in an uproar, the result, Papa would retreat to the quiet of his study, and Mary would pen a letter to Charlotte Collins asking if she might visit. With her plain looks and meager dowry, Mary had long since accepted the inevitability of spinsterhood with relative aplomb. The only bright spot in her dull existence were her visits to Kent where, much to Charlotte's relief, she and Mr. Collins happily discussed religious texts and the reverend's Sunday sermons. Unchanged was Lydia's primacy on the list of her mother's favorites, and because of this, only Mama would be happy by the turn of events.

Elizabeth decided not to dwell on Lydia's problems. Instead, she would concentrate on Kitty, who was again with child by her husband Joseph Wilkins, a curate serving with his father, the rector of Meryton parish. When the elder Mr. Wilkins passed on, Joseph would take over his father's position. Although the income was merely satisfactory, Joseph was most agreeable and very good to his wife.

With Palazzo Bardi now in view, Elizabeth understood why the count was so dismissive of Le Torri Dorate. From the front, it appeared that the palazzo, the color somewhere between yellow and orange, was twice the size of the Darcy villa and that did not take into account the two wings added to the rear of the building that framed the rear gardens. The ground floor of the villa was a colonnade with twin staircases leading to the main entrance. A pediment supported by a series of Tuscan columns accentuated the beauty of the first floor. Centered above the pediment was the coat of arms of the original owners of the villa, the Donatis.

Standing between the two arms of the staircase, waving to the occupants of the carriage, was Count Roberto Bardi. When the conveyance came to a stop, a servant in livery opened the door for the count's guests. As soon as Alexa's feet touched the gravel, she ran to Signor Roberto, who swept the child up into his arms and swung her around and around. After he had finished, he offered to do the same for Cassie, who readily accepted. It was but a minute before Alexa mentioned Sugar, the pony her father had bought for her soon after their arrival in Florence.

"Yes, Sugar is waiting for you," the count reassured her, "and we have Snowball for Cassie, and here is Antonio to take you to the stables."

With the children occupied, Count Bardi gestured for the ladies to enter the villa through the colonnade so that he might show them the tile flooring.

"This is how I make my money," he said, pointing to the floor. "When it comes to tile, I have done everything except pull the limestone out of the earth. I have cut and polished and bound the tile in crates for shipment. I have acted as a salesman traveling with my bound catalogs like an itinerant peddler. And do you know who my best customers are? The English, with their great country houses and fancy townhomes. And who, amongst the English, is my very best customer? Your new king, George IV. My tile is in every one of his houses, of which there are many. But I am different from most of His Majesty's vendors. I get paid!"

The count explained that unlike the English, there was no stigma attached to a man who earned his wealth in trade. The fortunes of many of the great families of Florence had come from the wool trade, and the Medicis had served as bankers to Europe for two centuries.

"The word 'office' comes from the Italian. Can you think what it is?" Elizabeth shook her head. "Uffizi," he said with a laugh. "The Uffizi served as the offices of the Medici. Second only to their love of money and the power it gave them was their love of art."

After climbing an interior staircase, they entered the public area of the palazzo. It was very similar to Le Torri Dorate in layout, the biggest difference being the size and number of rooms. Because the count's family traded in tile, each room of the public area had a different tile, and Jane and Elizabeth recognized the beautiful Breccia limestone of the entrance hall at Le Torri Dorate.

The last room to be revealed was the dining room, and the reason was obvious. Not only were the floors marble, but the walls as well. Centered on a palette of Carrara marble were various inlaid motifs featuring vases, fountains, nymphs, and other artistic designs in the numerous colors found near Florence. The artistry was exquisite.

Pointing to the various panels, the count explained that the dining room was his showroom. "When I want to sell tile, I bring the customer here, and he can see all that is available. No one leaves without buying something," the count said, laughing, "including Mr.

Darcy, who is to re-tile the front entrance of his country home in Derbyshire. Mr. Darcy drew up the plan, which is to feature a beautiful rosette; Mrs. Darcy chose the colors."

"You knew Mrs. Darcy?" Jane asked.

The count hesitated. "Although I was in her company on a number of occasions, I would not say that I knew her as she was a very private person. Like my wife, Mrs. Darcy preferred the company of a small group of intimates, mostly family. On those occasions when I was invited to Le Torri Dorate, I enjoyed Mrs. Darcy's company very much. Not only was she beautiful, but her playing on the pianoforte was heavenly, so much so that I replaced the pianoforte at the villa with a superior instrument so that I might better enjoy Vivaldi's *Spring*."

Jane knew how generous the count had been. She had declared the pianoforte to be the finest instrument she had ever had the privilege to play on, and there was rarely an evening when she did not entertain the residents of the villa.

"Perhaps you do not know that I am Mr. Darcy's landlord and that everything in the villa belongs to me," he said, laughing. "Mr. Darcy is currently enjoying the villa on a sublease from Sir Walter Greenwood, who returned to England because of family matters, but he will be back. He told me it is his intention to die in Florence as it is the nearest place to heaven on earth!"

"Such high praise," Elizabeth said, "but not undeserved. I know it will be difficult for me to leave."

"Then you must stay, and you must talk Mr. Darcy into staying—at least for a while longer!"

"I am not in a position to influence Mr. Darcy's decision either way," Elizabeth said, blushing.

"I am surprised to hear it. He spoke so highly of you and values your opinion above all others."

"That is because I am acting in the capacity of governess for his daughter."

"It is true that the gentleman wishes for you to love his daughter as much as he does, but Mr. Darcy is more than a father. He is a man!"

An uncomfortable Lizzy thought it best to change the subject. "If I may, Count Bardi, I would like your opinion on a personal matter regarding Alexa."

Elizabeth mentioned that the child's recollections of her mother were fading and that she was doing what she could to refresh her memory before it was too late.

The count shook his head. "You are already too late." When Elizabeth and Jane exchanged looks, Count Bardi offered an explanation for what appeared to be a heartless comment. "When my wife died, my grief was so profound that my family feared I might go mad. But over time, the pain lessened. Why? Because the memories of my most beloved Annunziata have faded. If this had not happened, it would have been impossible for me to go on living, and I must live because there are so many who are dependent upon me for their livelihoods. Although I have no children of my own, I am godfather to twenty-seven children. I must be here for them.

"So to answer your question, Miss Elizabeth, I do not believe that it is necessarily a bad thing that Alexa's memories of her mother are fading. It is part of God's plan to spare us a life of grief. If it were not so, the child would be consumed by sadness."

"Do you think what I am doing is unwise?"

"No. It is not unwise, but in the end, Alexa will cling to those memories that are most important to her, for example, her mother reading stories to her in her bed. When Alexa came to Palazzo Bardi, she would tell me about it."

Elizabeth felt a twinge of guilt. Her efforts on Alexa's behalf had been to supplant the memory of her mother always being in bed with those of her walking or drawing in the garden, but if the child had shared this particular memory with Count Bardi, then it was obvious it was a pleasant recollection and one she did not wish to forget.

"It is possible that Alexa will mention the times when her grandparents came to the villa for a visit," Count Bardi continued. "When in the company of her mother and father, Mrs. Darcy was a different person; she laughed and sang, and on occasion, danced. Her happiness made her even more beautiful than she already was. I remember the one time she attended a reception at the British Consulate. She moved about the room as if she was walking on a cloud, and people looked upon her as something of a goddess."

"Mrs. Darcy was a guest in my home for four days," Jane said, "and I do agree that she was perfectly lovely."

"Mrs. Darcy reminded me of Botticelli's *Primavera,*" the count said, "especially her gaze, a look of slight disinterest, as if the worries of the world were of no concern to her. However, if you wish to form an accurate picture of the lady, I advise you not to listen to what Signora Ciampi has to say. She is very biased."

Jane and Elizabeth again exchanged glances. Even Count Bardi recognized Signora Ciampi as a gossip.

"I see how you look at each other," he said. "I shall tell you that nothing can be kept secret from the signora as she is related by marriage to my housekeeper, Signora Parisi, and to Signora Moncini, the housekeeper at Le Torri Dorate, and both are related to half of Florence."

Anticipating their question of why he would maintain a friendship with a gossip, he explained that it was due to his fondness for her husband, who was much more than his notario.

"Signora Ciampi's father, Mr. Featherstone, was the buyer for the largest importer of Italian tile in England, and a man who would slash ten to twenty percent off my invoices stating, untruthfully in my opinion, that the tile had been irreparably damaged in shipment. In order to cut my losses, I sent Signor Ciampi to England to inspect the tile when it arrived in London.

"Because Ciampi was lonely, I arranged an introduction to Mr. Featherstone's plain daughter, whose Italian and bookkeeping skills were excellent. Ten years ago, Ciampi said that he had had enough of England and wanted to come home where the sun did not hide. I set him up as my notario, and he became my eyes in the city. Do not mistake his quiet demeanor for stupidity. He is always watching, always listening. Out of respect for Signor Ciampi, I tolerate his wife and her cutting remarks, but that does not mean that I have to invite her into my home or use my influence to secure an invitation for her to the Consul's receptions. I have no more to say about the woman or my blood will start to boil."

Following a discussion of the panels in the dining room, Count Bardi suggested they walk to the stables by way of the gardens that were in the formal style, each hedge trimmed to perfection and every flower in full display, not a brown leaf or faded bloom to be seen.

* * *

After seeing to the children's nightly ritual, Jane and Lizzy retired to the terrace. Despite the warmth of the evening, they would have their hot cup of tea.

Before saying anything, Elizabeth looked about to see if there was any evidence of a lurking Moncini. She knew that Flora was with the children, but where was the English-speaking Mario? And why was he still at the villa? Acting in his capacity of valet, he should have gone with Charles and Mr. Darcy.

"Lizzy, you are being silly. Mario is here because he is our driver. If you let your imagination run away with you, I shall find you looking behind the furniture for spies."

"I just wish I could remember what I said within his hearing."

"It certainly was not a declaration of your love for Mr. Darcy!" Jane said. Elizabeth quickly put a finger to her lips. Although Jane was improving, here was evidence that her mental confusion had not completely dissipated.

"I think we should go to your room, Jane. I am uncomfortable speaking in so exposed a space."

While taking the pins out of her sister's hair, Elizabeth mentioned the comments made by Count Bardi regarding Mrs. Darcy. "Jane, I am sorry to say it, but evidence is mounting that Mrs. Darcy either could not or would not be happy unless her family was about her, and by her family, I mean Mr. and Mrs. Cantwell and her sister Eugenie."

"Is it not possible that Mrs. Darcy used all of her energy to rally for her family's visit, and when they departed, an exhausted hostess was in need of rest?"

For Jane's peace of mind, Elizabeth chose to accept her sister's explanation. It was obvious that she was growing uncomfortable with the similarity of her story to that of Mrs. Darcy's.

Elizabeth also thought about what Count Bardi had said about allowing memories to fade. Had she not done the same thing with Mr. Darcy? Because she had come to regret her decision to reject his offer of marriage, she had jettisoned the most hurtful memories of their time together, clinging only to those scenes where they had come very close to actually enjoying each other's company.

Chapter 23

At breakfast, Jane discussed the contents of a letter she had received from Charles disclosing that Mr. Darcy and he were en route from Fiesole to Florence, thus reminding the ladies that their time in the City of Flowers was drawing to a close.

"Shortly after Mr. Darcy and Charles return from the Palio, the British Consul will be hosting his reception," Jane said, "and after that, it will be time to begin our long trek home. Mr. Darcy has suggested that we sail to Marseille, and from there, that we should go by carriage to La Rochelle where we would book passage to England."

Elizabeth noted the sadness in her sister's voice. Even the contents of a letter from Mr. Rumford, the man supervising the construction of Bingley Manor, in which he had asked for directions for decorating the entrance hall, had failed to revive her spirits.

"Now that I have seen the dining room of Palazzo Bardi," Jane said, "my ideas for decorating the public rooms have completely changed, most especially for the entrance hall. Maybe I should ask Mr. Darcy to help me with the designs."

Elizabeth thought it a good idea. With his interest in architecture, she was sure he could help, especially when one considered that he had already executed a design for his foyer. But with Mrs. Darcy's passing, she wondered if the plans for re-tiling the entrance hall at Pemberley would proceed.

"As soon as Charles returns, I shall think on the matter," Jane said. "In the meantime, we must visit Florence, and I have a plan."

Jane suggested that in order for Elizabeth to enjoy her day in the city, it was necessary to keep her away from Signora Ciampi. Jane's plan called for her sister to spend the day with the signora's husband. While Elizabeth and Signor Ciampi viewed Ghiberti's bronzes, Jane would go to the Uffizi with his wife.

"It a very generous plan, but one that requires that you spend the afternoon with Signora Ciampi, and that is not fair to you."

"But it is fair to *you*. You take so much pleasure in visiting Florence's treasures."

Thinking about a day without Signora Ciampi gossiping in her ear, Elizabeth could not resist. "It is a generous offer, Jane, and one I cannot refuse."

Through Mario, arrangements were made for the children to go horseback riding at Palazzo Bardi. While Alexa and Cassie were thus engaged, Elizabeth and Jane would go into the city. If luck were on their side,

Signora Ciampi would have a head cold and would be unable to join them.

* * *

By the time the campanile rang out the fifth hour of the afternoon, Elizabeth, under the direction of an English art student, had studied every panel of Ghiberti and Pisano's bronze panels and was waiting for Jane to appear. When she did, hard by her side was Signora Ciampi. How well the afternoon had gone was evidenced by Jane's expression. She reminded Elizabeth of someone who had sucked on a lemon. No sooner were the ladies rid of the gossiping signora and her kind husband, then Jane vented her frustration.

"That is the meanest woman I have ever met. She has very little to say that is kind about anyone, including the Moncinis and Parisis, and if I spoke Italian I would tell them so, but she reserves most of her snide comments for Mrs. Darcy. With no encouragement from me, she availed herself of every opportunity to speak ill of the lady. I shall give you an example. We were viewing a painting of that saint, you know, the one who is shot full of arrows..."

"St. Sebastian."

"Yes, he is the one, and Signora Ciampi turned it in to an opportunity to speak of Mrs. Darcy's complaints of ill health."

"What did she say?" Although Elizabeth asked, she was not sure she wanted to know.

"According to the signora, because Mrs. Darcy had suffered from a severe fever as a child, she had been 'coddled' by an overly protective mother and sister. At the time Mr. Darcy and Amelie Cantwell were introduced, because her parents had gone to France to resolve a property dispute, Amelie was living with her sister and brother-in-law in Sussex. Apparently, with the mother gone, her health improved."

"I am very glad to hear that Miss Cantwell was in good health when she was being courted by Mr. Darcy."

"I agree, but that was not what Signora Ciampi was trying to say. She was inferring that Mr. Darcy had fallen in love with an illusion, someone who bore little resemblance to the actual Miss Cantwell."

"Jane, who is to say that Mr. Darcy was not on *his* best behavior, and if that is true, should we now accuse him of presenting a false front so that he might win Miss Cantwell?"

Elizabeth was growing impatient with the whole notion of Miss Cantwell becoming engaged to Mr. Darcy under false pretenses. During courtship, was it not the purpose of the lovers to appear in the best light so that their suit might be successful? Thinking of her own parents, she wondered if it were truly possible for anyone to know the defects of one's partner before marrying.

"Jane, this is ridiculous, and I would like to know how Signora Ciampi knows all this? Was she there in Sussex when Mr. Darcy was courting Miss Cantwell? I can answer that question. I know she was not because she told me that since her arrival in Florence, she has never returned to England, so how on earth can she make such an accusation?"

"I have no idea. All I can tell you is that the signora was absolutely certain that her information is unimpeachable. Whenever I challenged any of her assertions, she always had a ready answer as if she had rehearsed it."

"Or had repeated it so many times that it has been committed to memory."

Jane nodded. "It was Signora Ciampi's belief that in order to make his wife happy, Mr. Darcy gave way in all things, including consenting to the lengthy visits of Mr. and Mrs. Cantwell. She stated that when the in-laws were in residence at Le Torri Dorate, Mr. Darcy spent most of his time with Alexa on horseback or visiting the Boboli Gardens or calling on Count Bardi because his mother-in-law took over the management of the house, and it irritated him greatly."

"These threads of gossip could very well be made up out of whole cloth." *Or she got her information from the Moncinis.*

"But I no longer care what that woman has to say," Jane said. "In a few days, Charles and Mr. Darcy will be home, and we will no longer be in need of the services of Signora Ciampi. And to that lady, I say good riddance!"

* * *

When the carriage containing Jane, Elizabeth, and the children traveled down the drive to Le Torri Dorate, sitting in front of the villa was the Darcy carriage, now covered in dust after its long journey from the north. As soon as the conveyance was sighted, the children let out a cheer at the return of their fathers. After scrambling out of the carriage, Alexa and Cassie ran up the steps of the villa where their heroes awaited them with open arms.

It was such a joyful scene that Elizabeth stayed in the carriage so that the families might enjoy their reunion. It was to last but a minute. With Alexa's hand firmly in her father's grasp, she led him to the carriage where he assisted Elizabeth from the conveyance. When his hand touched hers, she had to fight back her tears. She had never been so happy to see anyone in her life.

"You are very brown, Mr. Darcy," Elizabeth began.

"I am, indeed, Miss Elizabeth. If I did not have to sleep or eat, I would have spent the whole of my time out of doors."

"I am brown as well, Papa," Alexa said. "I have ridden Sugar these past five days."

"Only five! I have been gone nearly three weeks. I thought you would be at the stables every day."

"But we had to wait for Signor Roberto to return. Once he did, we went to Palazzo Bardi every day. That is why Miss Elizabeth is also a little brown."

Darcy studied Elizabeth's features and confirmed that Miss Elizabeth was browner than when he had left her.

"You must have removed your bonnet. I know you to be guilty because I once witnessed you doing such a thing during a walk in the meadows at Rosings Park."

"You have a good memory, sir."

"For certain things, I *do* have a good memory."

"Papa, Papa," Alexa said, tugging at her father's sleeve. "I have so much to show you. I have made sketches of Sugar and Snowball and..."

"You must be patient, Alexandra. I must first have a glass of wine to remove the taste of dust from my mouth, and I need a wash."

"After supper then, Papa. I have so much to tell you. We went to the Mercato Vecchio and bought the first grapes of the season, and we visited Signora Testaverde's gelato shop and..."

As Alexa dragged her father up the steps of the villa, Mr. Darcy turned around and gave Elizabeth a look of apology for his daughter's behavior, but she waved them on. In her mind, it was as it should be. Because they had been through so much together, they needed each other more than most fathers and daughters. She only hoped the second Mrs. Darcy would understand.

* * *

During supper, the children brought their wandering fathers up to date on all their activities. When Alexa and Cassie had exhausted every recollection, most of which involved ponies and kittens, Charles and Mr. Darcy shared their experiences in Pistoia and Fiesole.

With the admiration of a man who knows his horses, Charles related the events of the Palio. He was all praise for the skill of the riders and the athleticism of their mounts. Because the cloth prize had been won by the town's favorite, there was much celebration.

"The amount of wine drunk was prodigious," Charles related. "One man went so far as to lie under the tap of a wine barrel with his mouth open until pulled away to make room for another. I feared that with wine practically flowing in the streets, there would be fighting. With the exception of some pushing and shoving by a few young men, all went well. I have seen worse in London and with much less provocation."

After the Palio, the men had visited with a friend of Count Bardi's in Fiesole. Although their host had wined and dined his guests on the fruits of Toscana, their recollections centered on the ride in the hills where Florence and its Duomo could be seen in the distance. Charles was all praise for their host and the scenery.

"We stayed at an absolutely gorgeous villa. And from there you could see a Roman arena and Roman baths. I thought about you and Cassandra," Charles said, smiling at his wife.

"You probably thought of me because of the baths," Jane said, laughing, and everyone joined in.

"And I missed Le Torri Dorate," Mr. Darcy said, squeezing his daughter's hand, and then he looked at Elizabeth. "Although I went to Pistoia and Fiesole, my heart stayed here."

For Elizabeth, who was now so in love with Mr. Darcy that wherever he went, he took her heart with him, and in that way, she had been with him in Pistoia and Fiesole, and when he returned to England, he would travel with it as well.

Chapter 24

After supper, all adjourned to the terrace where the evening was filled with more stories of events in Pistoia and Fiesole with Charles the author of most and an amused Darcy providing confirmation of Bingley's retelling of scenes of vendors cutting pieces of cheese from huge wheels, bottles of Chianti in their straw *fiascos* hanging from hooks in the stalls, and most especially scenes of men walking through the streets wearing leggings, one leg red and the other white, which Charles insisted was a costume he would not wear "for a king's ransom." When that subject was at long last exhausted, Jane shared their evening at the Palazzo Bardi, most especially viewing the exquisite marble inlays in the dining room.

"Charles, you really must go to the palazzo to see these designs for yourself because words, no matter how descriptive, are inadequate. They are so very beautiful, and I would love to commission a rosette for the entrance hall of *Le Casa Bingley*." At the rechristening of Bingley Manor, everyone laughed, and Jane said that she was only half in jest. "I love the Italian language.

Everything sounds beautiful in Italian even the name of the fishmonger is beautiful, Signor Benito Antonucci, Pescivendolo. It is just... just so full of joy!"

Darcy laughed to himself. In addition to always smelling like day-old fish, Signor Antonucci was the grumpiest of old men, but he kept that to himself.

"I understand you designed a rosette for the entrance hall at Pemberley," Elizabeth said to Mr. Darcy.

"Yes, I did, but I have not ordered the tile as the colors are yet to be selected.

"Oh, I was told that Mrs. Darcy had chosen the colors."

"Yes, Amelie did offer some suggestions, but I think it only fair to wait until I marry again. After all, the future Mrs. Darcy will be living in the manor. Why should she not choose the colors?"

"Of course. That is perfectly reasonable," Elizabeth agreed.

"It is something to think about."

"Yes. It is."

After coffee, Jane and Charles said that they wished to retire and offered to supervise the nightly bedtime ritual Elizabeth had established for the children.

Once they were alone, Darcy offered to pour more coffee for Elizabeth, but she shook her head. "I find that coffee keeps me awake, and with the children so full of energy, I need a good night's sleep or they will get the better of me."

"Tea then?"

"No, thank you, sir." *Now that you have returned, I am quite content.*

After pouring a glass of wine for himself, Darcy asked Elizabeth what she had seen and done during his absence. At the conclusion of her summary, he indicated that he thought she would have spent more time in Florence.

"I was happy to stay at Le Torri Dorate with its beautiful views and lovely gardens, and Count Bardi has been so gracious. He has invited us to dine three times."

"The count did not talk your ears off?"

"He does enjoy conversation," Elizabeth said, laughing.

"The reason he talks so much is because he is lonely. He has six older sisters, and when all of the family congregates, there are so many children on the estate that it looks like ants swarming the hills. The count kindly sends for Alexa, and she is very sad when they leave, but nothing can keep the sisters in Florence during the summer. Count Bardi has said that there are only three types of people who will endure the heat of a Florentine summer: those whose business keeps them in the city, the insane, and the English."

"He is probably right," Elizabeth said while thinking of what she was willing to endure in order that she might view the treasures of the Renaissance, "but it is August and, yet, Count Bardi is at Palazzo Bardi."

"During the summer, when all his family goes north, he makes the rounds of the quarries to make sure all is well. Because his office is in Florence, he spends August examining the books kept for him by Signor Ciampi. In September, the first of the grape harvest begins, and he would not miss it as he makes his own wine."

"Yes, I know. We sampled quite a bit of it during our visits, and he explained the whole process."

"I assume you also spoke of art. Did he bring up the subject of the *Venus of Urbino*? It is one of his favorite topics."

Despite its name, the count had shared his opinion that Titian's masterpiece had nothing to do with Venus.

This painting is not about love, but about money and what it can buy. The Duke of Urbino is boasting to the viewer, everything in the painting belongs to me, the sumptuous fabrics, the palazzo, the woman. This painting is not about the Goddess of Love. This is about sex!

At the time of the count's exposition, Elizabeth had blushed a deep red, and Jane, a married woman, was only a shade paler, but the count did not hesitate to speak about something that would never have been discussed in a drawing room in England, at least not a drawing room in which Elizabeth and Jane were present.

191

When you speak of art, you must say what is in your heart. Too many English view art only with their eyes, and I ask, if that is your intention, why come to the Uffizi at all. Stay home and read a book about Titian! But if you choose to view this masterpiece, then you must let it enter your soul. You must be prepared to be consumed!

"I find the count speaks in superlatives," Elizabeth answered. "In his letters, I can easily imagine exclamation points at the end of all his sentences. He was most energetic when discussing the *Venus of Urbino*."

"And what did you think of the painting?"

"I confess I did not like it," Elizabeth answered truthfully. "I agree with Count Bardi, it is not about love, but is meant to appeal to the baser instinct of the male. To accomplish this, the artist uses a woman whose worth is determined exclusively based on her beauty and what services she can provide for the entertainment of the man who is paying her. To my mind, this Venus is being treated as chattel, and when her time has passed, she will be sold to another."

Darcy acknowledged that he did not like it either. "For the most part, I agree with you. However, the woman in this particular painting was independently wealthy, and she could have said 'no' to Titian. The choice was hers; she was not coerced. Whether she came to regret her decision, no one will ever know."

Elizabeth was uncomfortable with the conversation. Frequently, when Mr. Darcy spoke of art, she felt as if his opinions contained double meanings, ones that she did not understand.

"We were speaking of Count Bardi. I understand that there is another reason why he wishes to be in Florence in late summer. There is a festival on September 7 that he will not miss."

"Yes, the Festival of the Lanterns or *rificolona*," Darcy said. "It is a tradition of long standing and one in which peasants travel from the country into Florence from as far away as the mountains of Pistoia to celebrate the birth of the Virgin. In order to arrive at the church in time for Mass, these pilgrims must start their journey in the dark."

"And they would need lanterns to light their way," Elizabeth said, visualizing the progression of hundreds of humble peasants walking the dark, tree-lined roads of Tuscany.

"As they make their way from Piazza Santa Felicita to Piazza Santissima Annunziata, the pilgrims are guided by a cardinal of the church. After a great speech by His Eminence and a High Mass, the people celebrate into the early hours of the morning with food, drink, and song. Because the next day is a market day, they have brought in goods to sell: cheeses, honey, linen, yarn, and hand-crafted items, many of them carved from the wood of the olive tree. At the end of the evening, the paper lanterns are set ablaze. It truly is something to see. I hope I can convince the Bingleys to remain in Florence until that time so that you might see it."

"I think your efforts will be successful as Jane is reluctant to leave Florence."

"I do believe Mrs. Bingley has fallen under the spell of the *Venus d' Medici*."

"Yes, she has."

"And you, Elizabeth, are you reluctant to leave?"

"Yes," she said, her voice now a whisper.

"Why?"

She wanted to say, "I do not wish to leave because I am in love with you." There was a time when she could have said those words, a time in Kent when he had asked for her hand in marriage. But in the years between that time and now, he had fallen in love with another, a beautiful lady, and this woman, who, according to Count Bardi, appeared to walk on air, had given him a golden-haired child whom he adored.

"Why do you wish to remain, Elizabeth?" he repeated.

"There is nothing like Florence in England," she said, looking down at her hands. "And I shall miss Alexa."

"Arrangements can be made so that you do not have to say goodbye to Alexa."

Convinced that he was about to ask her to be his daughter's governess, Elizabeth stood up, and after saying a hasty "good night," she quickly left the room. She understood that before leaving Florence, he would ask her to accept the position, but not tonight. *Tonight the only thing I want to remember is Mr. Darcy saying my name.*

Chapter 25

"There is to be no dancing!" Jane said disappointed with Elizabeth's news.

"Mr. Darcy says that the reception area at the British Consul is too small for more than one or two couples to dance, and because of that, no one dances."

"I do so long to dance. We have not been to a dance since we left Aix," Jane said, pouting.

"It is because of the heat. Once the cooler weather comes, the dances will begin."

"Yes, but by the time they start in earnest, we shall be leaving for England."

After consulting with Darcy, Charles had set the date for their departure as September 9, two days after the Festival of the Lanterns.

There were few things that Elizabeth enjoyed more than dancing, and she, too, had been disappointed to learn that there would only be music at the reception, but she held up her hands to indicate that she was not in a position to do anything about the lack of scheduled dances.

"Well, what *do* they do at these receptions?" Jane asked.

"Apparently, they eat and drink quite a bit, and I have been informed that there is an excellent pianoforte in the room. I hope you will be asked to play."

Jane shook her head. Like Elizabeth, she was not comfortable performing in front of strangers. "But I think *you* should play. You play as well as I do."

"I definitely do not," Elizabeth protested, "and please spare me any false praise. I know where my talents lie." In the Bennet house, Mr. Bennet had declared that Jane's playing was "expertly done," Elizabeth's was "well done," and Mary's was "best undone." Kitty and Lydia had escaped their father's biting wit only because they had never learned to play.

"If you will not allow me to compliment your playing," Jane said, "then you will at least agree with me that your voice is superior to any of our acquaintance?"

Elizabeth had received enough compliments to know that she possessed a superior alto, and her mind returned to a time when she had performed at Lucas Lodge. While singing, she had been aware that Mr. Darcy was watching her, but decided that his purpose was to find fault. Instead, he had truly admired her talent and had told her so at Rosings Park. *No one admitted to the privilege of hearing you, can think anything wanting.* If only she had been less eager to think ill of him, things might have turned out differently.

"Have you decided what dress you are to wear, Lizzy?"

Knowing that an invitation to a reception at the Consulate was coveted, Elizabeth had given much thought to her choice of gown. There was a second, more important, reason why she had chosen so carefully. It was the only time she would be at a formal event with Mr. Darcy, and she intended to look her best. Her choice was a simple pale green gown with a wide sash beneath the bodice that served to accentuate her slender figure. At her final fitting, the dressmaker had paid her the ultimate compliment: "Because you are so beautiful, it is not necessary to add anything to the dress." Having always been in the lovely Jane's shadow, Elizabeth relished the compliment.

"I was sure you would pick that one," Jane said, nodding in approval. "If Mr. Darcy wears his dark-green coat, he will complement you beautifully."

"I was thinking the same thing," and Elizabeth laughed at their amateur plotting.

"In my opinion, you have made a good start in capturing Mr. Darcy's attention. Now all you have to do is remind the gentleman of the many reasons he fell in love with you in the first place."

"I only wish Charlotte were here, so that I might ask her how she succeeded in securing Mr. Collins—and so quickly. I am running out of time!"

"That is advice you *do not* want!"

The sisters broke out into laughter, but then the realization that there was so little time left dampened the mood.

"Oh, Jane!" Elizabeth sighed. "I really do not think I can do this. I have no talent in using arts and allurements to capture the heart of a man. I do not know how to flirt."

"You flirted with Edmund Long."

"That was ten years ago! And the only reason I flirted was because I was secure in the knowledge that he was not in a position to make me an offer. If I had thought there was any chance of his actually proposing, I would have fled the ballroom!"

"Lizzy, you do not need to employ arts and allurements. You need only be yourself—just more so. And remember that you once succeeded in having the gentleman fall in love with you, and at the time, you did not even like him. Now that you *do* like him, your task will be much easier."

That is easy for you to say.

With the Consul reception but two days away, all talk was dedicated to that subject. Even though they would not be attending, the children were practically giddy in speaking about it as both Alexa and Cassie had an interest in fashion. In fact, Elizabeth had consulted both when choosing her dress, and the two had endorsed her decision to wear the green one.

After supper and with the children settled in their bedchamber, Mr. Darcy took the opportunity to thank Elizabeth for what she had accomplished with Alexa.

"Before your arrival, my daughter would have clung to me, pleading with me not to go to the reception, and in all likelihood, I would have given in to her pleas."

"As much as I enjoy the praise, I am beginning to think that Cassie has had a greater effect on Alexa than I have. The other night, when you said how much she enjoyed spending time with Count Bardi when he hosted family gatherings, it gave me pause. I believe your daughter has been longing for the company of children, and because there was none to be had, she clung to you."

"I do believe I have been demoted from god to demigod."

"Not at all. You retain your place in the pantheon, but it is only natural for a child to want to be with other children."

"Yes, of course. I remember how eagerly I looked forward to my cousins, the Fitzwilliam brothers, coming to visit, and Anne de Bourgh as well. When Anne was a child, she was in much better health and had no difficulty in keeping up with her male counterparts. That is another reason why I wish to return to England. I want Alexa to know her cousins, Georgiana's children."

"You will have your wish soon enough. After the reception, your attention will turn to your departure for England, as will mine."

"You should not sound so sad about leaving Tuscany," Darcy said. "You once told me that you never thought you would come to Florence, but here you are. And you have not yet seen Venice or Pisa or Rome or Pompeii. They are but a few reasons for you to return."

Elizabeth laughed at the Master of Pemberley's ignorance of her financial situation, but she had no wish to end the evening on a sour note.

"I understand that in Naples there is a lottery where great sums of money may be won."

"Yes, I have played the game in Venice as well as in Naples."

"How much did you win, Mr. Darcy?"

"How very optimistic of you to think that I won."

"Well, if I should win the lottery, I would use the money to return to the Italian peninsula with a destination of Venice or Rome. But rather than travel home through France, I should like to go by way of the Alpine countries as you are to do. With it being so hot in Florence, I envy you the coolness of the mountains."

"What you are suggesting is not impossible."

"Oh, but it is. Charles is eager to return to Derbyshire so that the manor house may be completed. As per your suggestion, he goes by the quickest route."

"But Bingley is not the only one returning to England."

Chapter 26

While Elizabeth sat at her dressing table, Alexa and Cassie were sitting on the bed giggling. After witnessing the completion of Jane's preparations for the Consul reception, they had come to watch Elizabeth's transformation from governess to belle of the ball. Count Bardi had arranged for a cousin of his housekeeper to come to the house to do Jane's hair as well as her own. Before her marriage, Angela had served as a lady's maid to a contessa and was quite capable of taming Elizabeth's curls, and she had come prepared with a small chest filled with the most beautiful combs and jeweled hairpins. When she had finished, she declared Elizabeth to be *molto bella*.

"*Molto grazie*," Elizabeth said, pleased with the results, and she pressed some coins into the woman's palm.

Cassie, lisping in imitation of her toothless friend, suggested that her Aunt Elizabeth use the rouge that the woman of Paris wore and which her mother was now wearing, but Elizabeth would not.

"Your mother is much fairer than I am. In fact, I have been told by a certain Miss Darcy that I am brown, and as such, I am not in need of face paint."

"Then you must color your lips," Alexa insisted.

"As you wish." Elizabeth applied a layer of Rigge's Liquid Bloom, providing just a hint of rose.

"Papa will be very pleased," Alexa said. "When I told him that your dress was green, he said that he would wear his green coat."

Not knowing how to respond, Elizabeth asked Alexa to hand her her gloves. As she was putting them on, Jane entered the room.

"Oh, Elizabeth! You are absolutely stunning. You look as if you have a halo of stars in your hair."

"How lyrical, Jane, and I thank you. I must admit that I do not look too bad for someone who is soon to be eight and twenty."

"Pish posh! You will have every old goat at the reception staring at you."

Mr. Darcy had warned the ladies that the average age of those invited to the reception was about fifty, some of whom had wandering hands.

"I look forward to winning the admiration of any gentleman, no matter his age. At the dances in Meryton, I have become something of a wallflower as the requests now go to the young girls from the village, and rightly so. However, if any gentleman makes me an offer of marriage, I shall give it due consideration, especially if it allows me to continue to live in Florence."

When the ladies joined the men in the drawing room, they were smoking cigars. As soon as Charles saw his wife, he catapulted out of his chair and rushed to her side.

"My goodness, Jane, you have outdone yourself. I shall have to spend the evening fighting off the men."

Jane, obviously pleased by her husband's reaction to her considerable efforts, smiled broadly.

While Charles continued to laud his wife, Mr. Darcy was standing silent, staring at Elizabeth.

"You look very handsome, Mr. Darcy," Elizabeth said. And he certainly was in his dark green coat, cream waistcoat, breeches, and Hessian boots. She was quite convinced that there was no one more handsome in the whole of Italy than the gentleman from Derbyshire—at least of a certain age.

"I find myself at a loss for words," Darcy said.

"A thank you for the compliment I paid would suffice, sir."

"I was not referring to your compliment of *me*, but to how beautiful *you* look. I am surprised at how frequently you misunderstand me."

"Any compliment, no matter how excessive, is welcome," she answered, blushing.

"Certainly, you are not suggesting that I am lauding you with false praise. You know me better than that, so please allow me to say that you look even more beautiful than the night of the Netherfield ball, and at that time, I considered you to be one of the most handsome women of my acquaintance."

After allowing for the full weight of his words to settle, she finally thanked him.

"I have my faults, Miss Elizabeth, as you well know, but I always speak the truth."

* * *

With a quarter moon hanging like a scythe in a late-August sky, the Darcy carriage arrived at the British Consul fronting the River Arno. After climbing a staircase with only wrought-iron work as decoration, they entered the reception room of the consulate, a long, narrow room with an ornate gilded border outlining the ceiling, picture frame paneling with neo-classical embellishments, and a wood parquet floor. They were greeted by Sir Martin Spencer, who had been representing His Majesty's government in Florence for more than a decade. His elegant attire and confident pose identified him as a son of the aristocracy.

Having enjoyed Bingley's company in Pistoia, Sir Martin renewed their acquaintance with a hardy handshake for Charles and a gentle squeeze of Jane's gloved hand. He graciously thanked Mrs. Bingley for parting with her husband so that they might enjoy the Palio.

"My husband could not be kept from it. He has thought of little else since Mr. Darcy first mentioned it months ago," Jane answered. "He is in your debt for making the arrangements."

"It is always a pleasure to assist a fellow Englishman, especially when my efforts result in my attending such an enjoyable event. I confess I love a good race. When in England, I am a faithful attendee of Epsom Downs and St. Leger."

While Elizabeth listened to the exchange, she thought how much of this man's life was taken up with these brief exchanges, ones in which he must establish an immediate connection with a person or risk giving offense. He was good at his job, and he proved it with his warm greeting of Mr. Darcy before addressing Elizabeth.

"And you must be Miss Elizabeth Bennet of Hertfordshire," he said, taking Elizabeth's hand.

"I am, sir," Elizabeth said, curtseying.

"I have heard much about you."

"Yes, my brother-in-law is very generous in his compliments."

"Yes, he is, but he was not my only source," he said, and he looked at Darcy.

With those in line pressing in behind her, Elizabeth found that she need not respond, and she quickly moved into the room and went to Jane's side.

"What a gracious host Sir Martin is," Jane declared. "And so very handsome and tall. In my mind, I had pictured a portly gentleman who enjoyed his Chianti and pasta too much."

Darcy was correct in estimating the age of the Consul's guests and their reaction to a woman under the age of thirty. With their wives engaged in complimenting each other on their choice of fashion, the gentlemen flocked to Elizabeth's side, many openly flirting with the only unmarried woman under fifty in attendance. A jocular older man declared that with the exception of Elizabeth and Jane, everyone present had only recently escaped from a fossil exhibit at the archeology museum.

With such a press of people in such a confined space, Elizabeth made her way to the terrace for some fresh air, and she was soon joined by Sir Martin who exacted a promise that she must sing *The Ash Grove*.

"Mrs. Bingley has already committed to accompany you."

"It will be my pleasure, sir, but I must warn you, because I have not sung the tune in many years, I may be unsteady in my delivery." Elizabeth recalled that it was that particular song that had earned Mr. Darcy's praise. "Is *The Ash Grove* a favorite of yours?"

"I do enjoy hearing it, but the request is made by another," his gaze settling on a man who looked as if he had jumped out of a Cruikshank cartoon: short, round, with wisps of hair scattered about his head, and someone who was dwarfed by Mr. Darcy, who was standing behind him.

"I understand that before the Palio, you were enjoying the cool breezes of Lake Garda," Elizabeth said.

"Yes, how fortunate for me that I have a friend who owns a retreat on the lake. My wife and I spent ten wonderful weeks there." At the mention of the Consul's wife, Elizabeth lowered her eyes. "Despite rumors to the contrary, Lady Spencer is not in exile in England, but visits the Continent whenever the circumstances of overseeing our properties in Sussex permit. After all, one of us must earn a living!"

"Has Lady Spencer been to Florence?"

"Oh my, yes! Louisa spent a good portion of her youth here in Florence, as her father once served the old king in the same position I now hold with His Majesty, that is, until Napoleon forced him to take flight in 1805. My wife rarely visits, her preference being the cooler venues of the mountains. She finds the heat, amongst other things, intolerable."

In the reception room, Elizabeth heard the first notes of a song and recognized the tune as one of Jane's favorites. Despite her reluctance to perform, someone had coerced Mrs. Bingley into playing, and Elizabeth was glad of it as she loved to listen to her sister play. During Jane's recovery following Cassie's birth, it was one of the few exercises permitted by her physician. As a result, her playing was such that even Lady Catherine de Bourgh would have regarded her as a proficient. There would have been no comments about Jane being sent to the housekeeper's room for more practice.

With Jane nearing the end of the piece, Elizabeth felt the first flutter of nerves, and she remembered the first time she had exhibited in public when she was fifteen years of age. Although her audience was all known to her, she recalled how nervous she had been. To steady her nerves, her Great Aunt Susan had suggested that she find a friendly face amongst her listeners and to pretend that that person was the only one in the room. Her eyes had settled on her father.

While Jane arranged the music sheets, Elizabeth looked for Charles, her friendly face in the crowd. As he was engaged in a conversation with a man about a horse, his favorite topic above all others, she was unable to catch his gaze. While scanning the throng for another, her eyes settled on Mr. Darcy, whose calm demeanor she found reassuring.

Down yonder green valley where streamlets meander,
When twilight is fading, I pensively rove,
Or at the bright noontide in solitude wander
Amid the dark shades of the lonely ash grove.

'Twas there while the blackbird was joyfully singing,
I first met my dear one, the joy of my heart.
Around us for gladness the bluebells were ringing,
Ah! Then little thought how soon we should part.

Throughout her performance, Mr. Darcy's eyes never left Elizabeth, and she held his gaze. While looking at the gentleman, she thought how appropriate that she should be asked to sing a song where the lovers parted. Like so much of what she had experienced in

Florence, it was art reflecting reality. Overwhelmed by a sense of sadness, after responding to the warm applause of her audience, Elizabeth sought the privacy of the terrace. Because the iced cream was now being served, she found she was alone, but only for a minute, as Mr. Darcy soon joined her.

"Do you not like sweets, Miss Elizabeth?"

"I do, Mr. Darcy. But at the moment, I wish to settle my nerves. That is the first time I have performed in front of a room full strangers. I was so nervous that my voice cracked at the start of the second stanza."

"I find that accomplished people are often overly critical of their own performances. I can assure you that you did not crack. Your performance was exceptional. May I suggest a walk by the river as a way of settling your nerves?"

While holding her hand, Darcy led Elizabeth down a rear staircase that took them to the promenade fronting the river where other couples were enjoying the sublime scene.

"Are you enjoying the reception, Miss Elizabeth?"

"I am. My only regret is that there is no dancing. I do so love to dance."

"Until the grapes are gathered and the olives pressed, there is little time for dancing, and so none is scheduled. But once the harvest is completed, then the festivities begin. Every year, during the second week of October, Count Bardi hosts a gala, and it is one of Florence's premier events. You have visited Palazzo

Bardi. Can you imagine it filled with guests dressed in their finery and arriving in gilded carriages?"

"Gilded carriages?"

"Some of these conveyances are more than a century old, and the Florentines were never shy about showing off their wealth. During the gala, you must also picture the formal gardens of Palazzo Bardi lit with a hundred torches. It is as if the hills are on fire. It is too bad you will not be here to enjoy it, especially since it is the intention of the count to introduce the waltz. Have you heard of the dance?"

"Count Bardi has mentioned it, but I must confess that from his description it sounds scandalous."

"Why? Because the man puts his hand on the woman's waist?"

"It is my understanding that his hand remains there for the whole of the dance."

"That is because the man is actually holding the woman in his arms."

Imagining being in Mr. Darcy's arms, Elizabeth felt a warmth spreading throughout her body, but such a thought and its effect would remain hidden because she would never have the pleasure of being held in Mr. Darcy's embrace.

"I have never danced the waltz," Mr. Darcy said, a statement that brought Elizabeth back to earth. "Because of the intimacy of the dance, I would have to be in love with my partner."

And you are not in love with anyone.

In the distance, Elizabeth noted a flash of lightning and used it as an opportunity to change the subject. "I do hope it rains. The last storm provided much needed relief from the heat."

While she watched the approaching storm, Darcy watched Elizabeth. He would have liked to have said more about the waltz as the mere thought of holding Elizabeth Bennet in his arms was affecting him. What would be his reaction if he actually felt her hard against him? But such a conversation took place only between lovers.

"Whenever there is a thunderstorm, I find I have a visitor who stands about this high," Darcy finally responded and held his hand at chest level, "and this someone speaks with a lisp."

"Cassie is the same way. When you were in Fiesole, we had quite a storm. Following the first clap of thunder, I had two visitors come into my room," Elizabeth said, relieved that they would no longer be speaking of a man holding a woman in his arms. If she were to see Mr. Darcy dancing the waltz, she thought her heart would break as that would be a sign that he had fallen in love.

"You are so very good with the children," Darcy said.

"I find that I enjoy this age very much as I love their curiosity."

"And their curiosity leads to an endless series of questions, most of which arise shortly before the lamp is to be dimmed."

"Yes, that is true, but in a few short years, there will be no bedtime rituals. Their childhood will be behind them, and all efforts will be directed toward their coming out. But, for now, they live each day without a care in the world."

"I remember the end of my own childhood. It was when I left Pemberley to attend Winchester. I was absolutely terrified, and with good reason. I was leaving the loving home of my parents, where I could do no wrong, to go to a place where I could do no right. I remember wash buckets with a thin layer of ice on the top and eating watery gruel and the coal being doled out as if it were gold. More than anything, I remember always being cold."

"While you were eating your boiled oats, your future dance partners were learning how to embroider, paint tables, mend purses, sing, dance, curtsey, play a musical instrument, and learn a modern language, all so that they might catch the eye of a gentleman in possession of a good fortune."

"Yes. I do believe that the demands placed upon young ladies by society are too onerous."

"That was not always your opinion."

"No, it was not, and I know you are referencing our conversation at Netherfield concerning what constitutes an accomplished lady. I remember declaring that I knew only a half dozen such ladies. Do you recall your response?"

"I wondered at you knowing any."

"Exactly! Your wit, once again, served to skewer one of my more pompous statements. But what I said was an accurate reflection of my own experience. There *were* only six such ladies within my circle of acquaintances. Later, when I thought of who they were, I realized that although they were all so very accomplished, they were also very dull."

"From what I hear, one of those accomplished ladies is your own sister, Mrs. Legh. Of course, I am not suggesting that your sister is dull."

Darcy laughed at Elizabeth's postscript. "I can take no credit for Georgiana's natural talent or amiable disposition. However, it fell to me to supervise all the arrangements necessary for her debut. I came away convinced that moving an army into battle requires less preparation. I imagine it will be little different when it comes time for Alexa. It would be most helpful if there was a loving hand at Pemberley to guide her."

"I am sure there is no shortage of those qualified in England to fill that role," Elizabeth said, and then turned her eyes in the direction of the Consul. "We had best return to our friends."

Chapter 27

After an encore performance by Jane and Elizabeth, the evening came to an end. Mr. Darcy had not exaggerated when he had said the food and wine would be excellent, the Buontalenti cream superb, and the company entertaining. Elizabeth, who would listen to anything concerning Florence, found great enjoyment in hearing stories told by men and women who had come to the Tuscan city for a visit, but who had never gone home, many of them risking detention as enemy aliens during Napoleon's occupation of northern Italy.

With the smell of rain in the air, the carriage climbed the hill to Le Torri Dorate with Jane Bingley providing the commentary for most of the journey.

"You enjoyed yourself this evening, Mrs. Bingley," an amused Mr. Darcy said.

"I did, sir," Jane answered with a giggle and confessed that she had enjoyed the Chianti as well. "As a result, I am feeling a bit tipsy."

"For my wife," Charles said, taking Jane's hand, "it only takes two glasses of wine, and tonight she had three."

"The Chianti *was* excellent," Elizabeth agreed. "I enjoyed a second glass as well."

"Sir Martin has an arrangement with the Verrazano family to supply all his Chianti. He has a similar agreement with a family in Parma for their cheeses, and the fish is as fresh as you will find anywhere in Florence as it sent by express coach from Livorno. When you dine with Sir Martin, you are assured of an excellent table."

After arriving at the villa, Elizabeth immediately went to the children's room where they shared a bed with Flora Moncini.

"The approaching storm must have frightened them," Elizabeth whispered to Mr. Darcy who had followed her into the room.

"I am sure of it. It seems we arrived home just in time as I can hear the raindrops beginning to fall. Do you enjoy listening to the rain?" Elizabeth nodded. "Then before you retire, will you join me for a nightcap in the drawing room?"

"And what may I ask is a nightcap?"

"A nightcap is a drink that one enjoys before retiring. It first came to my attention when Sir Martin used it when we were together in Pistoia. He tells me that it is gaining in popularity in London's men's clubs."

"I imagine that when I return home, I shall find that much has changed as I have been gone for more than a year!"

As Elizabeth entered the drawing room, she realized how much she loved this room because it also served as the villa's library. On its shelves were numerous books about art and history. Although most were in Italian, they were beautifully illustrated, and with a cursory knowledge of Latin, she was able to puzzle out the inscriptions below the pictures.

"There is another reason I asked you to join me," he said, pouring two glasses of wine. "I wanted to apologize."

"Apologize? For what?"

"For leaving you in the clutches of Signora Ciampi while Bingley and I enjoyed the Palio. It was pure selfishness on my part," Darcy explained and handed Elizabeth a glass of Chianti. "I could not leave two women unattended at Le Torri Dorate without knowing that someone was looking after them. Before my departure, I left instructions with Signor Moncini and Mario that you were not to go into Florence unless Signor Ciampi had been notified."

Elizabeth already knew this. Because Mr. Darcy felt it necessary to apologize, obviously, he recognized just how awful the man's wife was.

"I did not realize that my request would prevent you from visiting Florence. When you told me that you had gone into the city on only a few occasions, I knew why: Signora Ciampi. She has a well deserved reputation as a gossip, and her tongue reaches into most houses in Florence."

After that remark, Mr. Darcy hesitated, and Elizabeth could see that he was unsure if he should proceed. In his eyes, she watched his struggle, and by her open countenance, she hoped to reassure him that she could be trusted.

"Among those who incurred the signora's wrath was my wife," Darcy began. "On several occasions, I told Amelie that if only she would invite Signora Ciampi to her salons that the gossip would cease. But Amelie would not, saying that it was very much like feeding the squirrels in Hyde Park. No matter how much you gave them, they always wanted more.

"And what was the grist for her gossip? My wife's health complaints. Were they real or, as Signora Ciampi would have you believe, all in her mind? I shall tell you that there was just enough truth in her stories to make believers of her audience."

"Mr. Darcy, I do want you to know that Jane and I did our very best to turn the subject away from your wife, but the only way to stop Signora Ciampi was to avoid her company altogether."

"I certainly believe you."

"And may I add that you owe me no explanation."

"I know that as well. Perhaps that is why I want to tell you a few things that might dispel some of the more malicious rumors about Amelie."

"I shall listen to anything you wish to share."

Darcy gestured for Elizabeth to take a seat on the sofa, and he sat beside her. "In order for my story to make sense, I must go back to a time before we came to Florence."

Darcy explained that Mr. Cantwell, Amelie's father, was His Majesty's representative in Bordeaux. It was his responsibility to make sure that the tax man would have his proper share once a shipment reached England. His position afforded him a handsome living, so much so, that he had successfully won the hand of a wealthy daughter of a vicomte who owned vast properties outside the city. When, in 1792, it became necessary for the family to flee the violence of the anti-aristocratic mobs, they had sailed to England. Once there, they settled in Sussex where Amelie was born. From their location on the English side of the Channel, they remained ever hopeful that the situation in France would improve and that they would recover their properties.

"In 1814, when Napoleon first abdicated, Mr. and Mrs. Cantwell immediately returned to Bordeaux. Because they had invested so much time and effort in seeking the return of their properties, even after Napoleon began his march to Paris the following year, they would not leave France. Amelie and their daughter, Eugenie, who was married to a French émigré, remained in England as guests of Sir James Pitcairn, a friend of my father, whose wife was also French. With so many French aristocrats settled in the South of England, they felt quite at home and formed their own social circle. It was at Sir James's home that I met Amelie. We were first introduced in June and married in September, and a year later, Alexandra was born. Although my daughter arrived early, she was healthy and hearty and has always been so. I am truly fortunate in that regard.

"However, that was not the case with Amelie as Alexa's birth had been difficult, leaving her quite weak. On the advice of her physician, Amelie, Alexandra, Eugenie, and I journeyed to Spa, where my wife's health and spirits showed considerable improvement. Several months after our return to England, Eugenie's husband, who was then in Grenoble, wrote to ask his wife to join him as he had been successful in recovering most of the property that had been confiscated at the time of the overthrow of the monarchy.

"It is important for you to understand that Eugenie and Amelie had never been apart, and with her parents now living in France, my wife was unhappy. In order to lift her spirits, I agreed to take her to Bordeaux. Since this was the first time I was in the company of my in-laws, I was ignorant of the overbearing nature of Mrs. Cantwell; that changed as soon as we were introduced. Before our bags could be unpacked, my mother-in-law insisted that Amelie was very ill and that we must immediately remove to the spa at Pau. When I suggested my wife's poor health was a case of *mal de mer*, I was subjected to a recitation of a series of childhood illnesses, the most serious of which was a bout with rheumatic fever. According to Mrs. Cantwell, Amelie's sickly childhood explained her fragility and lack of appetite. It was difficult to argue the point as my wife's appetite was poor, and because she was so thin, she appeared frail.

"Rather than speculate, I decided that I would seek expert medical advice, and so from Pau, we went to Montpellier where there is a medical college. It was found that Amelie had an unusual heart rhythm, a result of the rheumatic fever she had experienced as a girl. The doctor suggested that it would be best if we lived in a warm climate so as not to tax her heart."

The news of his wife's condition and its cure had sent Mr. Darcy reeling. Although he knew that Amelie had been less than enthusiastic about living in Derbyshire, a place so far removed from London and her friends in the South, it had never occurred to him that the beauties of Pemberley would be denied him because of his wife's health concerns.

"Because Pemberley is so much a part of me, I did not understand how it had failed to capture my wife's affections as well. But before leaving Spa, I had agreed to Amelie's request that we should go to Paris. Although my wife had never before been to France, I saw in her eyes a love for her ancestral home, and I understood that the happiness I experienced when I was at Pemberley would not be shared as her heart belonged to France."

This statement was said with such sadness that Elizabeth thought she might cry. Having visited the gardens at Pemberley and having seen the Georgian manor set amidst a beautiful park, she could easily believe that his inability to visit his estate had cost him much.

"After leaving Montpellier, we took up residence in Aix. It was decided that we would winter there and spend the summer with her sister in Grenoble. Any decision regarding a possible return to England was postponed.

"When in Grenoble, I received a letter from my brother-in-law, Christopher Legh, who had kindly agreed to manage the estate in my absence. The letter stated that there was unrest amongst the workers in Derbyshire, and he reported that on adjacent properties, some vandals had destroyed threshing machines and set fire to hayricks. I had never had any problems with my tenants and thought it best to return to address their concerns. I left behind Amelie and Alexa in Grenoble.

"After reassuring my tenants that no one would be thrown off the land and after visiting with Georgiana and her husband, I made my way south to Dover so that I might rejoin my family. Along the way, I stopped in Kent to visit with Lady Catherine and Anne de Bourgh. It was to be a visit like any other, and I had no expectations of experiencing an epiphany, but that is exactly what happened.

"After several days spent in the company of my aunt and cousin, I became convinced that Anne's illnesses were imagined, but unconsciously done, as it was her only defense against my aunt's overbearing personality. In this, she was assisted by her lady's maid, Mrs. Jenkinson, who acted as her protector, a role also played by Amelie's sister Eugenie when her mother came very near to overpowering her. With that observation, everything changed.

"So what exactly *did* I know about the nature of Amelie's health? From the doctor at the medical college, I had a professional opinion that my wife did have an impaired heart that denied her participation in more athletic pursuits, such as riding and vigorous dancing, but was she as sickly as her mother claimed? After careful observation, I came to the conclusion that if Amelie remained with her mother that Mrs. Cantwell would make an invalid of my wife. When I returned to Grenoble, I told Amelie that we must go back to England. I promised that her health would be the determining factor in any decision as to where we would live and that we could travel between London and Weymouth, where I own a seaside villa, and my country estate in Derbyshire, so that she might enjoy the best of England's weather. Her parents and sister were always welcome, but we *must* go home."

Before returning, Mr. Darcy, a student of art, architecture, and history, wanted to visit Florence. A visit to the Tuscan city would delay their return to England for at least a year, and for that reason, Mrs. Darcy had consented to the plan.

"Whilst in Florence looking for a villa where we could spend a few months on holiday, I visited with an old family friend. After having lived in Florence for nearly three years, Sir Walter Greenwood had to give up the lease because of finances. Without a moment's hesitation, I offered to take up the lease for a year, and I sent for my wife and child. Mrs. Cantwell soon followed."

Whenever Mr. Darcy spoke of his mother-in-law, his tone changed, and Elizabeth had no doubt that his decisions regarding his wife had resulted in a struggle between mother and son-in-law. *Poor Amelie! Poor Mr. Darcy!*

"Being enthralled with Florence and with my daughter, who went with me everywhere, at first, I made no objection to her staying with us. But Mrs. Cantwell's presence, during frequent and prolonged visits to our villa, only confirmed my belief that she was an impediment to my wife's recovery. With my patience sorely tested, I insisted that Mrs. Cantwell leave Florence. Immediately thereafter, Amelie suffered a collapse. Although I appeared hard hearted to my wife, I insisted that we adhere to our plan to return to England. We were to begin to make our way home in April, but that winter..." And he stopped. "So the question remains, were my wife's complaints legitimate or imagined?"

"Perhaps a little of both," Elizabeth said, "but that makes her little different from the most of humanity. We all like to be looked after."

"Elizabeth, I am very cautious about making promises, but to those whom I love, they can be assured that they will always be looked after."

Chapter 28

With their departure date approaching, the travelers went about their days with a sense of urgency, and Darcy suggested that the children's lessons be abandoned so that everyone could devote their time to seeing the delights of Florence. At supper, when the next day's itinerary was discussed, the adults and children listed their preferences. Charles wished to ride, Jane wanted to visit the *Venus*, and Cassie and Alexa were keen to pay a visit to a master toymaker in the Mercato Vecchio. Elizabeth stated that just being in Florence was sufficient to satisfy her. But all these plans were made before the arrival of Count Bardi.

"I would like to take you all to the pleasure gardens of Villa di Pratolino where we shall have a picnic!" the count exclaimed.

This suggestion was met with silence by Cassie and Alexa. They had visited enough gardens, and what were gardens when compared to a toy shop?

"Oh, this is not just any garden, but a magical garden." Now the count had their interest.

"Magical," Cassie said. "Will we be able to fly?"

"One never knows," the count answered in a hushed voice.

His instructions for the outing added to the mystery. Everyone was to wear their plainest clothes, and it would be necessary to bring a change of clothes for the children and a second pair of shoes for everyone. Signora Parisi would take care of everything needed for a picnic.

As the gardens at Pratolino were more than an hour's carriage ride from Florence, the picnickers left at first light. With the children riding with Charles and Jane, Elizabeth and Mr. Darcy shared a carriage with the count and his friend, Allegra Valdagno, a beautiful lady in her mid thirties. From the way the count looked at her, Elizabeth believed that she was someone who was much more than a friend to the count.

During the ride, Darcy tried to get Count Bardi to reveal why the gardens at Pratolino were now somehow magical. Shortly after his arrival in Florence, Darcy, Amelie, and Alexa had picnicked in the gardens, enjoying its artificial grottoes and one of Tuscany's most famous statues, the Colossus of the Apennines by Giambologna. Although pleasant, the gardens were hardly magical, but the count refused to give up its secret.

At supper, when Darcy had mentioned the colossus, Bingley had groaned. "I confess that if I see one more statute, I shall go mad. As it is, I cannot go to sleep without dreaming of Perseus cutting off the head of Medusa or that awful man carrying off the Sabine woman." Darcy had assured him that this particular statute was unlike any other he had seen.

On the way to Pratolino, Count Bardi provided a history of the villa that had been built for the Venetian beauty, Bianca Capello, the mistress of Franceso I, Grand Duke of Tuscany. Because so much of the art and history of Florence involved someone's mistress, Elizabeth no longer blushed at the mention of an *inamorata*.

Born into a wealthy noble family in Venice, Bianca Capello had fallen in love with a young clerk. Following a secret wedding ceremony, the lovers had fled to Florence. Eventually Bianca's beauty attracted the attention of the duke's heir apparent. Although married to Joanna of Austria, Francesco seduced Bianca with jewels, money, and other gifts, and she was more than willing to be seduced. To placate Bianca's husband, he was given a court appointment.

Elizabeth had read enough about the Medicis to know that they never left loose ends untied and doubted that things had gone well for Bianca's cuckolded husband.

"I am sure it is just a coincidence that her husband was murdered in the streets of Florence," the count said, "supposedly as a result of an enraged husband."

"Of course, Medicis never stoop to murder. The actual killing is always left to others," Allegra said, speaking for the first time, and Elizabeth understood why. Her English was heavily accented, but it only seemed to add to her charms, which were considerable, even when discussing murder.

"A few months after Joanna of Austria died," the count continued, "the grand duke married Bianca in a secret ceremony. In time, the marriage was made public, and she was crowned Grand Duchess of Tuscany."

"Is that all?" Elizabeth asked. With only the one murder, it seemed anticlimactic.

"Of course not! How boring that would be! History tells us that Francesco and Bianca died on the same day. Some say from malarial fever and others from poison."

"I suspect poison," Elizabeth said, and chuckled at how jaded she had become about anything to do with the murderous families of Florence.

The count declared that the first order of business was to eat. "*Mangia! Mangia!*" he said to everyone, and with the help of Mario and the Bardi driver, they set about laying out everything that Signora Parisi had packed for the picnickers.

It was a perfect day for such an outing, and with Mario chasing Cassie and Alexa, Elizabeth was free to savor the food and company without having to give any thought to entertaining her young charges. While enjoying grapes, cheese, and lemonade, Elizabeth declared that Jane and Charles must have a conservatory on their property so that they might have lemon trees.

"Do you have lemon trees at Pemberley, Mr. Darcy?" Elizabeth asked.

"We do."

"Jane, did you hear? There are lemon trees at Pemberley! I am sure Mr. Darcy will make a gift of lemons to the Bingleys once you are settled so that we might have lemonade all year 'round." And she laughed at her boldness in making such an assumption.

As she bit into a strawberry, Elizabeth declared that everything tasted better in Tuscany. The cheese was more pungent, the wine sweeter, the fruit always picked at the peak of perfection. She could not remember a time in her life when food had played a more important role, and the count declared that she was becoming Italian.

"With your dark eyes and beautiful thick hair, you could easily pass for an Italian," the count declared. "Do you not agree, Darcy?"

"I had not thought about it," Darcy said, "but, yes, Miss Elizabeth has beautiful dark eyes and beautiful dark hair. Whether Italian or English, Miss Elizabeth Bennet is beautiful."

"Thank you, Mr. Darcy," Elizabeth said, and she could not hide how pleased she was by his compliment. "I can see that the wine has loosened your tongue."

"I have only had the one glass," he said, raising it in proof.

"Drink up, Guglielmo," the count said to Darcy. "I am to unveil my magical surprise, and, ladies, please remove your bonnets."

At the center of the Pratolino Gardens was the footprint of the villa that had once served as the scene of

Francesco's wedding to Bianca. After years of neglect and vandalism, the building had been torn down, but the fountains and grottoes that had made the Pratolino famous remained.

Following the count's lead, the party walked to Cupid's Grotto and huddled together at its narrow entrance. With a flourish, Vicente, the count's driver, lit a torch and preceded the group into the grotto whose walls were covered with what looked like the dried lava of an ancient volcano. Although the grotto had been stripped of its statues, the fountain remained.

Mario called to the children to step closer to the fountain, and when they did, Vicente opened a tap that sprayed water into the air. The children, shouting and laughing, were soon jumping up and down in the mist. Wishing to share in their joy, Elizabeth stepped forward, and after taking hold of their hands, she led Cassie and Alexa in a little dance, and she was soon joined by Allegra. With little encouragement, the remaining adults joined the parade, the sound of their laughter reverberating off the walls of the grotto.

Chapter 29

As Elizabeth stood in the sun waiting for her frock to dry, she was joined by Mr. Darcy who declared that he would never get his daughter out of the grotto and that she might very well turn into a mermaid.

"Unless you see scales or the emergence of a tail, I would not worry," Elizabeth said, laughing. "Once Cassie and Alexa have finished, we will have them change out of their wet clothes, an option that is not available to adults in the party. Did you know about this, Mr. Darcy?" Elizabeth asked looking down at her wet frock.

"Honestly, no! I knew that at one time there were water automata here at Pratolino, but I thought with the villa in such a state of decay that the waterworks had suffered as well. Apparently not!"

Looking at Elizabeth, he was very glad that the automata remained in good repair. If he had known that a visit to the gardens would have resulted in seeing a wet frock clinging to Elizabeth's superb figure, he would have arranged for a picnic to Pratolino soon after her arrival.

Stepping next to her, he indicated that a hair was clinging to her cheek, and with his finger, he gently pushed the wayward tress from her face, wrapping it around her ear. For a few moments, nothing was said as the intimacy of the moment was savored, but the voices of the children reminded them that they were not alone.

"Well, I hope that the state of my petticoat, which is six inches deep in mud, will not invite censure as it once did at Netherfield Park," Elizabeth said as a way of breaking the silence.

"But you were not... I know you were not in the room when that comment was made," Darcy stuttered.

"It is true that I was not present when Caroline Bingley uttered those words. However, as a master of a great property, you should know that what is said above stairs is often repeated below, and from there, it makes its way to the ears of others. After all, the servants at Netherfield are friends of the Bennets, so all the time that Charles and you were at Netherfield Park, there were spies in your midst."

Darcy's face showed concern as he thought about many of the unkind comments he had made, not just about Elizabeth, but her friends, family, and neighbors. Were they, too, repeated? And was this another reason why he had been rejected at Hunsford Parsonage with such ferocity?

"You look alarmed, Mr. Darcy, but you should not be. That day, I looked positively wild, and if we had not been previously introduced, you would have been sensible to deny me entrance, and my petticoat *was* dirty."

"But did you hear my response to Miss Bingley's criticism?" Elizabeth shook her head. "In order for you to understand my response, I must make reference to another occasion. At Lucas Lodge, I mentioned to Miss Bingley the pleasure that a pair of fine eyes in the face of a pretty woman could bestow."

"Of whom were you speaking?"

"You, Miss Elizabeth. I was speaking of *you*!" Darcy said, shaking his head at her lack of understanding. "As I was saying. At the time of your arrival, Miss Bingley asked if your coming to Netherfield Park in such a state affected my opinion of your fine eyes, to which I replied, that they were brightened by the exercise."

"I wish the servants had chosen to repeat *that* comment rather than the one about my dirty petticoat."

"If they had, perhaps things might have turned out differently."

It was as if Elizabeth was struck dumb. She had no witty repost for Mr. Darcy because if "things had turned out differently," he would not have met Amelie Cantwell, the love of his life, and so she thought it best to ignore it.

With the children's shouts of joy serving as a background, Mr. Darcy and Elizabeth walked to the garden's most famous feature, the Appennino by Giambologna. Elizabeth did not know what to make of the crouching giant who appeared to be oozing rock. "I have never seen anything like it."

"This park was a designed by Buontalenti to be a fantasy land, and you must agree that the giant is fantastic. I only hope it survives the plans the Council has made for it. It has been decided that Pratolino is to become an English garden."

"An English garden! Why ever would they do that?"

"Since the conclusion of the wars on the Continent, more and more English are coming to visit. Many of them are looking for a bit of England right here in Tuscany."

Elizabeth had been told by Signora Ciampi that once the cooler weather arrived, the English emerged from their mountain retreats and descended on Italy's great cities "like a cloud of locusts," crowding the Uffizi and the piazzas of Florence.

"If what they want is a bit of England, then they should remain in England!"

"I agree. When in Rome, or, in this case, Florence, do as the Florentines do!"

After settling the matter, Darcy and Elizabeth continued along the path. As they walked, he mentioned that he had not been told that Signora Valdagno would be joining them. Because it was obvious that Count Bardi and Signora Valdagna shared an intimate relationship without benefit of marriage, Darcy was uncomfortable with Allegra being included in their group.

"Have the count and Signora Valdagno been together for a long time?" Elizabeth asked.

"I would guess about three years."

"Will they marry?"

"I doubt it. When her husband, a man of considerable wealth, died, he left her a substantial fortune paid out in yearly allotments. However, the will stipulates that if Signora Valdagno remarries, all payments cease."

Elizabeth understood Mr. Darcy's concerns, but she also understood loneliness. Each night, when Jane and Charles went to their bedchamber, they enjoyed an intimacy—a connection—that she would never know: the precious hours reserved for a man and woman in love.

"I think she is a delightful addition to our party," Elizabeth declared. "Had you met her before?"

Darcy's relief was evident, and he indicated that on a few occasions, he had ridden with her and the count at Palazzo Bardi.

"Signora Valdagno will stay with the count until his sisters return in October. At that time, it will be necessary for her to go back to Verona as they do not approve of the arrangement."

Allegra's situation put her in mind of another, and Elizabeth thought this might be the appropriate time to thank Mr. Darcy for all he had done for the youngest Bennet sister.

"Since we are speaking of family connections, I would like to acknowledge your kindness to my sister, Lydia. I only recently learned of your generosity."

Despite Darcy's apparent discomfort with the subject, Elizabeth thought that such a generous gift should not go unacknowledged.

"Your secret was betrayed by Lydia herself." She explained the circumstances under which Charles and Jane had learned of the quarterly allowance paid by Mr. Darcy. She also acquainted Mr. Darcy with Lydia's changed circumstances.

"I do not know what will happen to George Wickham as he is not allowed at Longbourn, or in Meryton, for that matter."

A year earlier, while visiting Hertfordshire, Wickham and Lydia had had a terrible row. An angry Wickham had visited the local public house, and in a drunken rage, had broken tables and chairs. The publican had sought compensation from Wickham's father-in-law. Although Mr. Bennet had agreed to pay half the damages, the owner was forced to absorb the remainder of the costs, causing hard feelings amongst neighbors.

"Now that the army does not want him, Wickham must make his way in the world, but he has no talents, no skills."

"Do not worry about George Wickham. He always manages to find someone to prey upon," Darcy said, practically sneering. "When one considers that he was perfectly willing to ruin the reputation of your sister, it is an example of Christian charity that your parents allowed him to cross their threshold." Then he paused. "Excuse me. I should have inquired earlier. I know that you have had a letter from England. Are your parents in good health?"

"They are, sir. My mother is as she always was, but for the first time in many years, my father is enjoying being a farmer. Last year, Charles purchased two pairs of breeding Gritstone sheep for him, and this enterprise has met with success. My father's letters are filled with little more than news about these woolly creatures."

Elizabeth suspected that this was a topic of interest to Mr. Darcy. During her visit to Pemberley, Elizabeth remembered the pastures were thick with sheep. "Are you familiar with the breed?"

"I am," he said with an uncomfortable look. "I think it is time that I lured Cassie and Alexa out of the grotto. They will need to dry their hair or they will be chilled on the ride to Le Torri Dorate."

While Mr. Darcy went in search of the children, Elizabeth rejoined Jane and Charles who were walking the path, arm in arm, like two lovers.

"Charles, where did you get the pairs of sheep you gave to Papa?"

"Sheep! My goodness! What a question on such a beautiful day."

"Did you get them from Mr. Darcy?"

In his letters, Mr. Bennet had mentioned the unique black and white faces of the Gritstone breed, and in her mind's eye, Elizabeth could picture those same sheep dotting the pastures of Pemberley. The sheep on the Bingley's leased property in Derby were of a different breed.

"I see Darcy has convinced the children to leave the grotto," he said, walking away from the sisters. "I shall look after Cassie," he called over his shoulder to his wife.

Charles's refusal to answer Elizabeth's question provided confirmation of her suspicions.

"Jane, why would Mr. Darcy buy our father two pairs of sheep?"

The only answer Jane could think of was taken from the Old Testament, a time when a man presented a woman's family with livestock.

"Jane, what on earth does that have to do with Mr. Darcy giving our father sheep? The tradition of which you speak was so that a man might secure the hand of a daughter in marriage."

"Yes, I know."

"That is ridiculous!" an exasperated Elizabeth said.

Jane offered her agitated sister a glass of lemonade, but she waved it away.

"Here is what I think may have happened," Jane continued. "After learning from Charles of Papa's financial difficulties, he made a generous gesture to help the family of the woman he had once asked to be his wife. If he was good enough to purchase a commission for Wickham and wedding clothes for Lydia, why not sheep for Papa?"

In a state of total confusion, Elizabeth leaned against a tree for support, her frustration so great that she thought she might cry out.

"Jane, I am mentally exhausted from trying to figure out what is going on in Mr. Darcy's mind. I must look for clues here and there as if we were engaged in some sort of parlor game. And these clues are so easily misinterpreted!"

"But if Mr. Darcy were not in love with you, why would he bother to leave clues in the first place?"

This comment gave Elizabeth pause for thought. "But what if you and I are wrong about Mr. Darcy? What if he bought those sheep for Papa as a demonstration of Christian kindness and had nothing at all to do with me?"

"Oh, Lizzy!" Jane said, seeing her sister's anguish. "I am so sorry for you."

"Sheep! Really, Jane?"

Chapter 30

With lessons for Cassie and Alexa suspended for the duration of their time in Florence, Elizabeth was packing up the books, pencils, and writing paper in preparation for their departure. With the children in the orchard picking lemons with the Moncini children, she used her time alone to concentrate on Mr. Darcy and rehearsed a speech he would never hear.

"My dear Fitzwilliam, although we must part, I am fortunate in that I have so many good memories of our time together here in Florence," Elizabeth announced to an empty room. "And the other day, when you touched my face at Pratolino, well, that will stand me in good stead until I am old, gray, and toothless." She put her hand up to her face in an attempt to recreate the moment.

"Hello there!" Elizabeth heard Mr. Darcy cry out, and she thought she would jump out of her skin. "Did I hear you talking to someone?" he asked as he entered the cellar. "Are you alone?"

"As you find," she said, her voice shaking. Had he heard what she had said? Apparently not, or he would have had a look of shock rather than puzzlement on his face. "Have you come to offer your assistance?"

"I am at your service, Miss Elizabeth," he said with an exaggerated bow.

"This pile," she said, pointing to a stack of books, "was taken from the library. It would be helpful if you would carry them up to the house."

After reaching the library and being relieved of his burden, Darcy asked Elizabeth if she would render an opinion on something he was planning to do at Pemberley.

"As I have previously mentioned, I drew up the plans for a rosette for the entrance hall." After removing a scroll from a shelf, he unrolled the paper to reveal a pen and ink sketch of his concept. "Is it too much?" Darcy asked of the complicated design.

"Not at all," Elizabeth answered while admiring the series of diamond-shaped pieces that made up the composition. "It is beautiful."

"I only wish you had visited Pemberley and not just the gardens. If you had, you would have seen that when you enter the house, there is a double wrought-iron staircase, very much like what you saw on the exterior of Palazzo Bardi. What I am hoping to achieve is the illusion of the twin staircase embracing the rosette."

"Then you have succeeded," Elizabeth said, nodding in approval. "Have you chosen the colors?"

"No, and that is where I need your assistance." Darcy described the colors of the entrance hall and asked what colors would complement them.

Without hesitation, Elizabeth reached for a book featuring some of the paintings and mosaics discovered in the ruins of Pompeii. "Because the foyer is yellow, I think these colors would look beautiful," she said, pointing to shades that could be found everywhere in Tuscany, most particularly rust, green, and yellow.

"Do you not think they may be too vibrant for an English country house?"

"You have asked for my opinion, and here it is. Every time you enter your home, you will have a reminder of your sojourn here in Tuscany. At a minimum, it will serve as a conversation piece."

"You have convinced me to proceed. If necessary, I shall have the entrance hall repainted or maybe I will raze Pemberley and replace it with a palazzo."

Both laughed at the idea of a palazzo sitting in the midst of Derbyshire. With the matter settled, Darcy shared a story his father frequently told of his visit to the buried city of Pompeii that he had viewed as a young man on the Grand Tour.

"According to his guide, Papa was very fortunate to be visiting the ruins just as the workers were excavating an important monument. He stood transfixed as the laborers removed the volcanic debris surrounding the hidden treasure, carrying away one wheelbarrow after another. My father was thrilled by the experience and wrote home to his parents to share his good fortune in being in the right place at the right time.

"Shortly after this auspicious event, my father departed for Capri for a lengthy visit, but before taking ship for Marseille, he wanted to revisit the ruins at Pompeii one last time. Lo and behold! He had arrived just in time to see the excavation of another monument. He could hardly believe that he had stumbled upon two important discoveries in his two visits to the ruins. Can you guess what had happened?"

"The excavation revealed the exact same monument your father had already seen unearthed?" Elizabeth answered with a question in her voice.

"Exactly! The whole thing had been staged as meticulously as any performance at Drury Lane and was done for the benefit of the many tourists who flock to Pompeii, most particularly the English, because we cannot get enough of Rome's glorious past."

"What was your father's reaction when he discovered the ruse?"

"He found it amusing. My mother, on the other hand, was outraged by the artifice practiced on her unsuspecting countrymen."

"Although I understand your mother's point of view, after all, those tourists *had* been deceived, I understand your father's as well. Despite the deception, he had watched some very clever people revealing Rome's history in a unique way. As a man of the world, he appreciated the effort required to stage such a scene. Either way, he was a witness to history."

Darcy started to laugh. "Your ability to see both sides of the equation is to your credit."

"If I am to be praised, then why do you laugh?"

"Because Alexa has told me that I must be more like Miss Elizabeth and be willing to listen to both sides of an argument."

"When I made that statement, I was hoping to make your daughter more receptive to opinions voiced by Cassandra who is at a disadvantage because of the year's difference in their ages."

"Alexa has learned a great deal from you."

"I certainly hope so as that was the point of the exercise." Fearing that this might lead to a discussion of her staying on as Alexa's governess, she moved in the direction of the library door. "Have I answered all your questions regarding the rosette?"

"Yes. Your advice is always excellent. I now feel confident in giving the commission to Count Bardi, who will contact the necessary people in England."

"Yet another reason for you to look forward to your return to Pemberley."

"Yes, and before I leave, I hope to have at least one other."

Elizabeth let out an exasperated sigh. "Mr. Darcy, I am greatly complimented by your high opinion of me, but I have already indicated that I have no wish to..."

The sounds of Cassie and Alexa's laughter filtered into the room, and their conversation came to an end. Although she had been unable to complete her sentence, surely her tone had indicated that this was a subject she had no wish to revisit.

That night, after giving the matter more thought, she understood why Mr. Darcy was so insistent on bringing up the subject of her being Alexa's governess. Until that matter was settled, he would not be free to seek a bride. With that realization, she lay down on her bed and cried until there were no more tears to be shed.

Chapter 31

It was long past midnight when Darcy finished his third glass of Chianti. Alone, and with a storm rattling the shutters, he had remained in the drawing room as the weather suited his mood. A good drenching might serve to wash away the thoughts that were denying him any hope of a good night's sleep. Elizabeth had seen to that.

At the time he had written to Charles to invite him to come to Florence, his hopes for a *rapprochement* with Elizabeth had been high. After her arrival in Florence, he had done everything within his power to show her that he was a different man from the Mr. Darcy who had proposed marriage so abominably in Kent. In the months following her rejection, her words had come to haunt him: "the last man in the world I could ever be prevailed upon to marry" and "if you had behaved in a more gentlemanlike manner." There were others, but those two in particular had cut like a knife.

In the ensuing months, his anger had concealed the depth of his wound, but anger soon gave way to despair. During the day, he was successful in banishing all thoughts of Elizabeth Bennet from his mind. It was the nights that proved tortuous. In his imaginings, he had taken her in every way possible. He had touched and tasted and savored every inch of her body, and his hands had provided her with as much pleasure as she had given to him. But then daylight came, and the space beside him remained empty.

Devoid of any hope of marrying the woman he loved, he had set out to look for a wife as he must have an heir. Shortly afterwards, he had been introduced to the beautiful, elegant, and accomplished Amelie Cantwell, a woman who seemed perfect for a man of his rank and situation in life. Enchanted by her beauty and talent, he had allowed himself to believe that he had fallen in love, but in his haste to take a bride, he had mistaken love for something very different. He soon came to understand that he had paid a high price for the occasional visit to Amelie's bedchamber.

Before their first anniversary, it was apparent how ill suited they were for each other. Behavior that he had once taken for shyness turned out to be a lack of curiosity. And he understood its cause. For the whole of her life, Amelie had been sheltered by her parents and sister, and even after their marriage, she showed little interest in anyone other than her family and a few trusted friends. As a wife, she did the minimum that was expected, but seemed incapable of providing the emotional nourishment her husband so desperately needed. As a result, he lived his life on the periphery.

His isolation was most keenly felt when Amelie's parents and sister came to visit. As they shared family stories, always in French and spoken with a Bordelais accent he found difficult to follow, he became an outsider in his own house, and in his loneliness, he had turned his attention to the bright spot in their marriage: Alexandra.

Darcy was aware that the closeness of his relationship with his daughter invited comment, but he did not care. When he was in Alexa's company, he was happy, and with his wife so aloof, so removed from the heart of their marriage, the love of his child was sufficient—must be sufficient—to ensure his happiness. But all that had been turned on its head when he had visited with Jane and Charles Bingley at Netherfield Park, a time when Cassandra was being led around by her nurse on leading strings.

Observing the domestic felicity of the Bingleys was painful enough, but it was nothing compared to the anguish he felt when Elizabeth Bennet entered the room. In this, their first encounter since his disastrous proposal at Hunsford, every sentiment, every feeling returned. His belief that he had banished her from his thoughts had been an illusion.

During the times when they were together at Netherfield, he had kept his distance, but distance did not prevent him from hearing the sound of her voice or, most particularly, her laugh. And in seeing and hearing her, he realized how much was lacking in his own marriage. Being a man of honor, it was necessary to remove such thoughts from his mind, and the only way to do that was never to see her again. When Amelie asked to visit her parents in Bordeaux, he agreed. Thus began the start of his exile from England.

After arriving in Florence, things had gone from bad to worse. The fantastic world of art that surrounded them was of no interest to his wife, and she rarely ventured beyond the gardens. When winter came, because Amelie felt the cold more keenly than most, she kept to her bedchamber. If Darcy and Alexa were to see her, they must go there. The excellent pianoforte that Count Bardi had sent to Le Torri Dorate sat silent, and with the exception of Christmas dinner and a celebration of Twelfth Night, the dining room and drawing room were all but abandoned.

It had been a gloomy enough winter, but then the entire household fell ill with influenza. While Darcy saw to Alexa's care in his room, it became necessary to send into the city for someone with immunity to the disease to nurse his wife. On the night his wife died, the nurse had come into Darcy's bedchamber to tell him that the end was near. Although in a fevered state, he had raced into her room, took Amelie's hand in his own, but in a matter of seconds, she was gone.

When Alexa recovered from her own bout with the influenza, she asked for her mother. For so young a child, it was as if Amelie had disappeared into the ether. In her fear that he, too, might vanish, she clung to her father, and in his unhappiness, he had allowed it.

And so it was until Charles Bingley had accepted his invitation to come to Florence, and with his acceptance came renewed hope that he might convince

Elizabeth that he was a man worthy of being loved. In that, he had failed miserably. If the children had not interrupted their conversation in the library, his plea to be her husband would have been outright refused—again.

Darcy's dark musings were punctuated by a thunderclap, and his thoughts immediately went to Alexa. Since his wife's death, she was terribly frightened of thunderstorms, and so he must go to her.

When he entered her chamber, he expected to find Alexa and Cassie sprawled helter-skelter across the bed, their coverings tossed about. Instead, he found them nestled amongst the blankets with Elizabeth between them. Apparently, when she had heard the storm approaching, she had gone into the children's room to comfort them.

As a gentleman, he should have withdrawn, but he found he could not. It had always been so. He was drawn to Elizabeth as metal to a magnet. It had been that way from that first meeting at Meryton. After refusing Bingley's suggestion that they dance, he had noted her fine eyes and light figure. By the time of her visit to Netherfield Park had ended, he had fallen under her spell. He had never been so bewitched, and he remembered thinking that if it were not for the inferiority of her connections, he would be in some danger. As it turned out, not *some* danger, but *great* danger.

Admiring the sleeping beauty, he felt ever fiber of his being respond. At no time in his life did he want anyone as much as he wanted Elizabeth Bennet, but then longing had been replaced by despair.

"Why, Elizabeth? Why will you not have me? I have changed." He could feel the tears welling up in his eyes. "I have tried so hard to prove that I am a good man—a man worthy of your love. I could make you happy. I already make you smile and laugh, and that would be just the beginning. I could show you the world. Please give me another chance. That is all I ask."

When Elizabeth stirred, Darcy retreated, and he realized that tomorrow was the Festival of Lights. If he did not succeed in convincing her to look upon him as a husband, all would be lost, and because he would never marry anyone other than Elizabeth Bennet, he would remain a lonely man.

Chapter 32

Elizabeth noted the date, September 7, the day the Florentines celebrated the *rificolona*, the Festival of Lanterns. Because it was a pilgrimage of faith, Count Bardi suggested that it was best to view the procession from the villa and leave the celebration to the devotees of Mary.

"And there is no better view than from the tower," the count added.

On several occasions, Elizabeth had climbed the steps of the tower, and on each visit, she recalled her first day at Le Torri Dorate when she had stood beside Mr. Darcy looking out at a then unvisited Florence. That night, the gentleman had come to her in her dreams, not as a rejected suitor, but as her husband, a dream that had recurred time and time again, only to meet with the harsh reality of a new day.

After supper, all the occupants of Le Torri Dorate, as well as Count Bardi and Signora Valdagno, adjourned to the front of the villa with its green expanse of lawn and unobstructed view of the city.

With a chest full of Chianti from the count's cellar and the children serving as outlooks for signs of the first torch, the adults waited for the hue and cry to be raised. When the first speck of light was seen, Alexa, Cassie, and the youngest of the Moncini children let out shouts of joy and came running to share the good news that the festival had begun. Below them, tiny bits of light moved in an unbroken progression on their way to the Piazza Santissima Annunziata where hymns of praise would be sung to honor the birth of the Virgin.

"For the best view, you should go up to the top of the tower," the count said to Elizabeth, "and Mr. Darcy should go with you."

Elizabeth hesitated, but soon found Jane beside her. In a whisper, Jane reminded her sister that tonight was her last opportunity to let Mr. Darcy know of her love for him. In Elizabeth's mind, the result of such a declaration would succeed only in making a total fool of herself, so much so that she would never be able to be in Mr. Darcy's company again.

Her reluctance was noted, and the count cried out "*Andiamo*! Why do you hesitate? Who knows what you will find once you reach the top."

Elizabeth finally agreed and walked ahead of Mr. Darcy. As she stepped out onto the balcony, the murmur of a thousand whispered petitions reached her ears, and she had no doubt she was viewing a religious commemoration that had changed little since the Middle Ages. The combination of the spectacle below and the knowledge that she would be leaving Florence in two days' time resulted in tears forming.

"It will be so difficult to leave here," she said to Mr. Darcy, and she could hear the break in her voice. "But I have no choice."

"You *do* have a choice."

Elizabeth sighed. Despite Jane's wishes and her hopes, it had never been Mr. Darcy's intention to entertain the idea of a courtship, and now she had run out of time. As such, she would allow Mr. Darcy to ask the dreaded question: "Will you be a servant in my household?" Despite her deep affection for Alexa, the answer must be "no."

"Mr. Darcy, first allow me to thank you for the honor of your offer, and I certainly understand your reasons for wishing to consider me for the position, but surely you must understand why I cannot accept?"

"In all honesty, no, I do not understand! In our months together here at Le Torri Dorate, I thought all former slights had been forgotten."

"I can assure you that all slights have been *forgiven*, but it is impossible for me to *forget* the past," Elizabeth answered. "When you consider that there was a time when you imagined me to be the Mistress of Pemberley, do you not see why it would be impossible for me to accept a position that will make me your servant?"

"My servant?"

"Yes, your servant. I know you would be a kind master, but my master nonetheless. So, no, Mr. Darcy, I must continue to refuse your every attempt to have me serve as Alexa's governess."

Darcy was stunned by her complete misunderstanding of his intentions. "You know, Elizabeth, for an intelligent woman, you get a lot of things wrong."

"Excuse me?" Elizabeth said, completely taken aback.

"Yes, wrong! When we were together in Hertfordshire and again in Kent, you failed to recognize my particular notice that led to my first proposal, and you have missed every clue, of which there were many, of my intention to make a second offer of marriage."

"Marriage? But nothing has been said about marriage."

Darcy shook his head and looked up into the sky before letting out a laugh. "Every time I tried to speak of it, you walked away. You did it yesterday in the library when I asked *you* to choose the colors for the rosette at Pemberley, a task that I had specifically mentioned would fall to my *wife*.

"As for the matter of you serving as Alexa's governess, if you recall, when you first suggested setting up the classroom on the estate, *you* referred to yourself as Alexa's governess, and I stated quite clearly that I could *never* think of you in such a way. And I ask you, how many times have I used the word 'wife' in your presence? I can answer that for you—too many to count—and why would I have done that if it was not my intention to make you an offer?"

"But when you spoke of 'wife,' I thought you were referring to Mrs. Darcy. I remember a particular time when you were together at Netherfield Park. You stood beside her and whispered in her ear, and she turned and gave you such a smile. Afterwards, she went to the pianoforte and played a piece so brilliantly that there were tears in your eyes. I had never seen anyone so in love as you were at that moment."

Darcy again shook his head. Here was another thing she had got wrong. "I remember the occasion of which you speak. A few minutes earlier, you and I had enjoyed a brief conversation. The reason for its brevity was because my feelings for you were so strong that I had to get away. I asked Amelie to play something so that my distress would not be noticed by everyone in the room. Amelie's smile was for the piece I suggested that she play. It was her favorite. And the tears? The tears were for you, Elizabeth. For what I had lost by your refusing me."

"I do not understand," Elizabeth said, shaking her head.

"I can see that. Perhaps when we last spoke of my wife, if I had told you everything, you would not now be confused."

After removing his coat, Darcy folded it and placed it on the top step of the tower staircase and indicated that Elizabeth should sit down, and he squeezed in beside her.

"After your rejection of my offer in Kent, I was very angry which, considering the tone of my letter, should come as no surprise to you. Because of the ferocity of your rejection, I knew that it was pointless to pursue you, and being of a mind to take a wife, when I met Amelie, I thought, why not Miss Cantwell? She was beautiful, had exquisite poise, and enough accomplishments to satisfy even Miss Caroline Bingley, with the added benefit that she was in no way—either physically or in temperament—like you. I wanted no lingering reminders of my feelings for you.

"I cannot answer for Amelie as to the reasons why she accepted me. Perhaps she found me handsome. I once heard her refer to me as that great, tall fellow. At the time, I thought it was a compliment, but now I am inclined to believe she was a little afraid of me. I know her mother, in correspondence with Amelie, encouraged the match because, at one and twenty, her daughter was facing the prospect of spinsterhood. The reasons no longer matter. The fact is that if we had taken the time to get to know each other better, we would never have stood in front of a priest exchanging vows to love, honor, and obey. Amelie did not love me, and I did not love her. I had hoped that would change as it had for my parents, but we formed no such attachment.

"After Eugenie's departure for Grenoble and our return to Pemberley, Amelie became seriously ill. Although every physician in the shire was consulted, no one could identify the cause of my wife's complaints. Finally, I sent to London for a doctor, and he advised me that my wife suffered from melancholia, and her symptoms were as real to her as if she had a physical malady. He suggested that I address the source of her unhappiness by visiting her parents in France. For a multitude of reasons, I agreed.

"You already know of my visit to Montpellier, but what I did not tell you was that while we were there, Amelie suffered a miscarriage. The doctor who cared for Amelie was associated with the medical college, and he informed me that because of my wife's fragility and 'narrow physique' that she should not have any more children as it might result in her death.

"I am not a heartless man, Elizabeth, but I am a man, and this news was, to say the least, unsettling. But I would not satisfy my needs at the risk of my wife's life. When Amelie recovered from the miscarriage, we traveled to Grenoble to spend the summer with her sister. After my trip to England to address the concerns of my tenants, I returned to Grenoble where I found Mr. and Mrs. Cantwell in residence. At first it appeared that everything was as I had left it, but something *was* different. During my absence, my wife had acquainted her father with the changed circumstances of our marriage.

"I knew from conversations with my father-in-law that Mr. Cantwell was inclined to take the Continental view of marriage, that is, an heir, a spare, and a mistress. This arrangement is certainly not unique to the French. My own cousin, Lord Fitzwilliam, has had a string of mistresses, and our king is little better than a hound in heat. What my father-in-law was trying to tell me was that I had Amelie's permission to take a mistress."

"Oh dear!" Elizabeth could not imagine such a thing. Matrimony was a holy sacrament. To agree to such an arrangement was a sin.

"Elizabeth, I am a man of many faults, but I can honestly say that when I make a promise or take a vow or swear an oath, I mean what I say. The arrangement suggested might well work for Mr. Cantwell and my cousin, but *I* am not an adulterer! From that day forward, we lived separate lives. The only thing that united us was our love for our daughter, and Amelie was content to have it so.

"Once we took up residence here at the villa, we maintained separate apartments, something Alexa was quick to take advantage of. I soon noticed that she would sneak out of her own room to share a bed with her mother. Eventually, it became a nightly occurrence.

"And so it was until the entire household was struck down with influenza. At Amelie's passing, I was overcome with grief, but not for the reasons you imagined. You see, Elizabeth, you have been under the wrong impression from the start. It was not that I loved Amelie too much. It was that I loved her too little." Turning to Elizabeth, he took her hand. "God forgive me, but I never stopped loving you. When we were at the top of the Duomo, I told you that I had loved once, but I was referring not to Amelie, but to you. Can you learn to love me, Elizabeth, because I am a man greatly in need of love?"

Elizabeth placed her hands on his face, and with a boldness born of love and heartache, she kissed him and kissed him again. "Fitzwilliam, I do not need to learn to love you. I am already *in* love with you!"

"Are you just saying that to make me feel better?" Elizabeth shook her head. "Now I am the one who is confused. You must tell me how this came about."

"I do not know exactly when I fell in love with you, but if I must choose a particular moment, it was when you took my hand in Livorno. I remember thinking, 'I am in trouble now!'"

"But when you were in Livorno, you did not even like me!"

Elizabeth shared with Mr. Darcy the change in her opinion from the time of their bitter parting at Hunsford. Believing Mr. Darcy continued to grieve for his wife, she was determined to conceal her true feelings.

"You said that when I took your hand that you were in trouble, and you are as there is no way of avoiding the question I am about to ask you," he said. "If there was more room, I would get down on bended knee."

"I shall make room," Elizabeth said, stepping back onto the tower balcony.

On bended knee, Darcy asked Elizabeth not just to be his wife, but his friend, advisor, and life's companion. "I want you to be with me everywhere and for all time."

"Fitzwilliam, I gladly accept your proposal and promise to be all those things and more if only you will love me forever."

After placing his hands around her waist, Darcy pulled Elizabeth close to him, and for a few minutes, he savored his ability to hold the woman he loved in his arms. But then his need to kiss her overpowered him, and he sought her mouth with a passion born of a thousand imaginings, and she responded in kind.

* * *

During their time in the tower, Elizabeth and Darcy had heard the cries of the children for them to come down, and when they finally did, they emerged holding hands. The eruption of joy that followed the announcement of their betrothal could be heard throughout the hills surrounding Le Torri Dorate, and Elizabeth wondered if the pilgrims below were thinking that their prayers were receiving a heavenly response.

Alexa, who had been so long without a mother, asked if she might call Miss Elizabeth "Mama."

"I would very much like that," she said, kissing the child.

The count immediately suggested that the marriage take place in the chapel on the Bardi estate. "I would invite Sir Martin to perform the ceremony, and for the honeymoon, I would suggest a visit to Rome and Pompeii and the Isle of Capri."

"But I was to return to England with Jane, Charles, and Cassie," Elizabeth said, failing to grasp the changes that had come with her acceptance of Mr. Darcy's proposal.

"Perhaps, Jane and Charles could alter their plans," Darcy suggested.

"I would gladly do so," Jane answered, "but I really need to begin the journey home. If memory serves, when I was carrying Cassie, I experienced considerable morning sickness around my third month."

"Jane, are you...?"

Jane nodded, and after taking hold of Charles's hand, she made the announcement that she was with child.

"Another reason to celebrate!" Count Bardi roared, and the wine glasses were refilled. Before the count could propose a second toast, a cheer arose from the city below, and the residents of Le Torri Dorate saw a thousand tiny flames shoot into the night sky as the lanterns of the pilgrims were set ablaze. The symbol was not lost on Elizabeth and Fitzwilliam.

Epilogue

During the glorious autumn that followed their marriage, before turning south to Rome, Elizabeth and Fitzwilliam were given passes to view the Vasari Corridor between the Palazzo Vecchio and Palazzo Pitti secured for them by Count Bardi as a wedding present. They also attended the Bardi gala where Elizabeth enjoyed the company of all those Florentines who had remained hidden during her time in Florence. It was there that the newlyweds danced their first waltz, and if it had not been known to all that they had married a month earlier, from the way they looked at each other and from the way Mr. Darcy held his bride, everyone in the ballroom would have seen that the couple was deeply in love.

The gala was followed by a visit with Alexa to Venice, a city that came very close to Florence in the wealth of its art.

At the conclusion of a visit to the Eternal City, the newlyweds and their daughter joined Colonel Fitzwilliam and his wife at their villa overlooking the Bay of Naples. All during the winter, they enjoyed visiting the sights of that city as well as several visits to Pompeii where they happened upon the discovery of a significant monument. Mr. and Mrs. Darcy rejoiced in their good fortune, just as the elder Mr. Darcy had done a generation earlier.

After so lengthy a separation, the reception at the Bennet residence was overwhelming. As soon as the carriage came down the drive, the doors of the manor were flung open, and the house was soon emptied of all its occupants, including Aunt and Uncle Gardiner.

Kitty was the first to embrace her sister and introduced the newest member of the Joseph Wilkins family, her baby son Thomas, named after Mr. Bennet, and their two-year old daughter, Francine, named after Mrs. Bennet.

Lydia, with three small people clinging to her skirts, stepped forward and took Mr. Darcy's hand and whispered, "You were right about George. I assume our arrangement will continue, but more about that later."

"Where is Marianne?" Elizabeth asked of Lydia's baby.

"With a wet nurse," Lydia answered. "I just could not nurse her any longer as she is a greedy little one and took everything I had. As you have never had a child, you have no idea how demanding they can be!"

"Well, we can discuss that later, Lydia" she said, giving her husband a sideways glance, and then stepped away from the crowd so that she might make an announcement. "Dear family, I would like to introduce you all to Miss Alexandra Darcy." And the child executed a perfect curtsey. Pointing to Lydia's children, Elizabeth informed her daughter that all the children gathered to welcome them were now her cousins, and the child's eyes grew wide at the idea of having so many new friends.

When Mrs. Bennet had her turn, her greeting was so effusive that it very nearly overpowered her son-in-law. Slipping her arm into his, she walked with Mr. Darcy into the house.

"Only yesterday morning, I was telling Lady Lucas how rich my Lizzy will be. What pin money, what jewels, what carriages she will have! Considering her age, I had quite given up on her ever finding a husband, but here you are in the flesh! I hope you will forgive me for having disliked you."

If permitted to speak, Darcy would have answered that there were no hard feelings. Having endured the manipulations of Mrs. Cantwell, he understood that his new mother-in-law, although lacking in decorum, was harmless. Besides, he could afford to be generous. Pemberley was a long ways away.

With Mr. Darcy held captive in the parlor, Mr. Bennet was able to properly greet his beloved daughter. "When we are alone, you must tell me how all this came about. You gave no hint of it in your letters."

"It will be easier to comprehend if you forget everything you knew about Mr. Darcy when he first came to Hertfordshire. I can assure you that he has no improper pride and is perfectly amiable. I love him so very dearly, and he is very good to me."

"If this be the case, my dear Elizabeth, then he deserves you. I could not have parted with you to anyone less worthy."

"Papa, there is another matter that you should know about." Elizabeth acquainted her father with her husband's actions on behalf of Lydia.

"Ah, so it was not your Uncle Gardiner who laid out so much money! His refusal to accept any repayment now makes sense. Of course, I shall offer to repay Mr. Darcy tomorrow."

"Papa, he would not wish it."

"But I must make the offer nonetheless. Of course, he will rant and storm about his love for you, and there will be an end to the matter." With the desired outcome achieved, father and daughter enjoyed a good laugh. "I must also thank him for the two pair of Gritstone sheep."

"But how could you have possibly known they were from Fitzwilliam?"

"Until I received your letter revealing your marriage to Mr. Darcy, I had not put two and two together, but I must say that I found Charles's gift to be a curious thing. He is as good a son-in-law as a father could wish for, but he knows less about husbandry than I do. The clouds cleared with your announcement. When I realized what Mr. Darcy had done with the sheep, I had a good laugh. It was downright Biblical. I had the urge to go out and purchase sandals and a staff," Mr. Bennet said, chuckling. "In all seriousness, Elizabeth, I think this ember has been burning for a very long time."

"You would be correct," she answered, kissing the cheek of her dear Papa.

* * *

After two weeks spent at Longbourn, the three Darcys began the journey toward Pemberley. As Darcy looked out at the familiar Derbyshire countryside framed within the windows of the carriage, he shared with Elizabeth stories about his neighbors and tenants, and his wife could see the delight in his eyes and the comfort it brought him to be amongst its familiar terrain.

When the carriage passed the porter's house, Darcy took hold of his wife's hand and kissed it. "I never thought this day would come, but here you are, my wife and the Mistress of Pemberley. Finally, after so many years of wandering, I have come home."

The scene staged at Longbourn was repeated at Pemberley. When the doors of the manor were thrown open, Georgiana and her husband emerged. Trailing behind their parents, were a tribe of children and a nursemaid holding the youngest Legh child. Georgiana was perfectly lovely and bore a strong resemblance to her brother. In temperament, she would prove to be open and affectionate.

Georgiana rushed to Elizabeth and kissed her cheek. "My dear sister, welcome to Pemberley, and, Fitzwilliam, how we have missed you." With her two hands, she pulled her brother's face to her own and kissed him on both cheeks. "I am delighted to be once again in your company."

Elizabeth thanked Georgiana for the warm welcome and declared that she was looking forward to the two sisters getting to know each other, and with Jane living nearby at the now completed Bingley Manor, she would be living in the midst of family.

"We have been very busy here at Pemberley," Legh said to his brother-in-law. "Quite overrun with workmen sent by Count Bardi to install your rosette, Darcy."

"Is it done?" Darcy asked, ignoring the false annoyance in Christopher's voice. It had been his hope that the remodeled entrance hall would be completed in time for Elizabeth's arrival, but Count Bardi would promise only that he would do his best and explained that "because these men are artists, they take as much time as is required. In the end, it is always worth the wait."

"This very morning, two workmen came to Pemberley to collect the last of their tools, and although Georgie and I have tasted enough dust to last a lifetime, the work is splendidly done. I have no doubt you will be pleased."

"My thanks, Christopher, and not just for the rosette and your stewardship, but for being so good to my sister."

"It is easily done as she is very good to me. And now for the unveiling!"

Darcy asked that Elizabeth close her eyes, and after steering her into the entrance hall, Mrs. Fitzwilliam Darcy had her first view of the interior of Pemberley Manor. And as soon as her eyes opened, she let out a cry.

"Oh, Fitzwilliam! It is far more beautiful than I ever... I do not know what... All I can say is that I shall be very happy here."

"Ah, at last, a complete sentence," Darcy said, laughing at his wife's expense.

Elizabeth was right. The rosette exceeded all expectations. The colors were brilliant and the design perfectly executed, but her eye was soon drawn to a niche, where a three-foot replica of the *Venus d' Medici* perched.

"You have sent home a bit of Florence," Elizabeth said, pleased to see the *Venus*.

"Do not grow too fond of her, my dear. It is actually a gift from Charles to Jane."

"I was hoping that Jane, Charles, and Cassie would be here."

Georgiana explained that the Bingleys were unable to come. The previous week, Jane had been safely delivered of her child, another daughter.

"As soon as I received word, I went to Bingley Manor," Georgiana explained. "I can assure you that all is well. Your sister was sitting up in bed taking nourishment and wanted you to know that this birth was nothing like Cassie's, and she looks forward to a visit from you at your earliest convenience."

"Oh, this is very good news. Jane has been much on my mind. What did she name her daughter?"

"Florence."

"Florence! Oh, that is too funny. In Tuscany, Florence is a boy's name."

"Your sister was aware of that, but because she attributes the return of her good health to her sojourn in that city, she wanted to name the baby for a place where she experienced a rebirth."

"Florence is the perfect name for her child," Elizabeth said. "And I shall tell you that Jane was not the only one who experienced her own personal Renaissance."

"Although the *Venus* is not for you, I do have something," Darcy said to his wife. "If you will follow me."

"Alexa, please stay here with me," Georgiana said, taking hold of the child's hand, and she put a finger to her lips. "Your Papa has a surprise for Elizabeth."

"Mama has a surprise for him as well," Alexa said. Mimicking her aunt, she put her fingers to her lips.

Darcy again asked that his wife close her eyes. Once they were in the drawing room, he told her that she could open them. Before her was a painting of her beloved Florence. The artist had captured the city as the sun lay on the horizon, casting a warm glow on the greatest city of the Renaissance. In the distance appeared Le Torri Dorate surrounded by the cypress trees that punctured the blue Tuscan sky.

"Fitzwilliam, this is the perfect gift as I shall have a reminder of the splendid summer I spent with you in Florence. I am quite overwhelmed," she said, and she began to cry. "I confess I have grown weepy of late."

"This painting is not for you alone. It serves as a reminder of how my plan to capture your heart succeeded."

"You have my attention, sir. Please continue."

"As soon as I learned that you would be traveling to Paris with the Bingleys, I was quite determined to lure you to Florence. First, I enticed Jane to visit Vichy and then Aix, and each change in plan brought you closer to me. I thought with such a setting as Florence that you might see me in a better light, and eventually, you would consent to be my bride."

"My goodness! If only you had thought to involve me in your plans, you would have saved both us much heartache. But no matter, in the end you succeeded, and with or without Florence, I love you so very dearly."

Looking at the painting, Elizabeth wondered if they would ever go back to the City of Flowers.

"Of course, we shall. Not any time soon," he said, laughing. "But I promise that we shall go back!"

At the door, they heard a soft knock made by a small hand.

"Come in, Alexa," Darcy called to his daughter.

"Did you tell him, Mama?"

"Tell me what, Alexa?" her father asked.

"You are not the only one with a surprise," Elizabeth said, "but I could not send mine ahead."

"No, she could not," Alexa giggled. "But she did bring it with her."

"Well, I am good and stumped. Where is this gift that traveled with me, but without my knowledge?"

Elizabeth took her husband's hand and placed it on her stomach. "Your child grows inside me." Darcy nodded and smiled. "Why do you not look surprised?" Elizabeth asked, looking at Alexa.

"No, it was not Alexa who gave away your secret."

"How long have you known?"

"Alexa, you may go and play with your cousins." After the little girl had skipped out of the room, Darcy pulled his wife into an embrace. "I knew it from the moment you conceived."

"Fitzwilliam, do be serious."

"I *am* being serious." Elizabeth gave him a doubtful look. "Do you remember the first night we were in England when we stayed with Aunt Catherine?" Elizabeth nodded. "After we made love, I knew. That is all I can tell you. I knew that you had conceived."

Elizabeth thought about it, and the time would be right.

"It was meant to be, Elizabeth. Although the road was painful, it was the only way I could have both Alexa and you in my life."

Now that they had come full circle, Elizabeth asked her husband to account for his having fallen in love with her all those years ago. "Did you admire me for my impertinence?"

"You ask that question as if your impertinence were a thing of the past."

Elizabeth ignored the gibe. "I believe I roused an interest in you because I was so unlike the other women of your acquaintance."

"That is certainly true. I cannot think of a single soul who taxed my patience more than you did."

Elizabeth punished him by removing his arms from her waist, but it lasted for all of a minute, and she was once again in his embrace.

"In truth, I cannot fix on the hour, or the spot, or the look, or the words, which laid the foundation. I was in the middle before I knew it had begun."

"That answer will suffice—at least for the time being. And, really, all things considered, I begin to think it perfectly reasonable. To be sure you knew no actual good of me, but nobody thinks of that when they fall in love."

THE END

Other books by Mary Lydon Simonsen:

From Sourcebooks:
Searching for Pemberley
The Perfect Bride for Mr. Darcy
A Wife for Mr. Darcy
Mr. Darcy's Bite

From Quail Creek Crossing:
Novels:
Darcy Goes to War
Darcy on the Hudson
Becoming Elizabeth Darcy

Novellas:
For All the Wrong Reasons
Mr. Darcy Bites Back
Mr. Darcy's Angel of Mercy
A Walk in the Meadows at Rosings Park
Captain Wentworth: Home from the Sea

Short Story:
Darcy and Elizabeth: The Language of the Fan

Modern Novel:
The Second Date: Love Italian-American Style

Patrick Shea Mysteries:
Three's A Crowd
A Killing in Kensington

Printed in Great Britain
by Amazon.co.uk, Ltd.,
Marston Gate.